P9-DGB-340

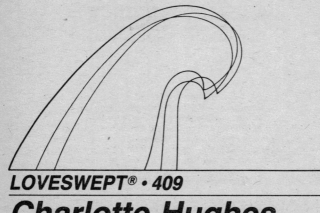

LOVESWEPT® • 409
Charlotte Hughes
Private Eyes

 BANTAM BOOKS
NEW YORK • TORONTO • LONDON • SYDNEY • AUCKLAND

PRIVATE EYES

A Bantam Book / July 1990

*If you would be interested in receiving protective vinyl
covers for your Loveswept books, please write to this address
for information:*

Loveswept
Bantam Books
P.O. Box 985
Hicksville, NY 11802

ISBN 0-553-44039-X

Published simultaneously in the United States and Canada

Bantam Books are published by Bantam Books, a division
of Bantam Doubleday Dell Publishing Group, Inc. Its trademark, consisting of the words "Bantam Books" and the
portrayal of a rooster, is Registered in U.S. Patent and
Trademark Office and in other countries. Marca Registrada.
Bantam Books, 666 Fifth Avenue, New York, New York 10103.

PRINTED IN THE UNITED STATES OF AMERICA

OPM   0 9 8 7 6 5 4 3 2 1

To D.J. with love

One

"Uncle Jeeter, I quit my job."

"Quit your job! When?"

"Ten days ago. But I should have quit long before."

"Is old man Hobsen still trying to get his paws on you?" Jeeter asked, his face etched with concern.

Ashley Rogers sighed heavily, her full lips sandwiched together in a tight frown. "He hasn't stopped trying to get me into the sack since my divorce became final four years ago. Once I made it clear I wasn't interested, he made my life miserable. I couldn't take it any longer. I should have filed sexual-harassment charges against him ages ago, but I thought I could work it out."

"I oughtta take him apart limb by limb—"

"He's not worth the trouble, Uncle Jeeter. Besides, I have more pressing problems. I've filled out applications all over Atlanta, but nobody will hire me. I think he's giving me a bad reference."

Jeeter Hamil reached across the desk and captured his niece's hand in his. He squeezed it comfortingly. "What can I do, sugar?"

Ashley smiled at the man sitting before her, despite the feeling of desperation that had settled in her gut since she'd walked out on her job, a job she'd held for six years. It hadn't been easy—it had gone totally against her character. And it frightened her, knowing she had two children to support.

"You have a job opening . . ." She held up the classified section of the *Atlanta Journal and Constitution,* where she'd circled in red his advertisement for help. "I'd like you to consider me for the position."

Jeeter gazed at his niece in mute surprise before he pulled himself up from his chair and lumbered across the room to a makeshift table that held an old percolator resting on a chipped hot plate. He poured another cup of coffee and offered her one, but she shook her head.

"I don't think you're cut out for private detective work, sugar," he began in a fatherly tone, once he'd settled back into his chair. "Besides, this ain't no kind of work for a woman."

Ashley rolled her eyes. "You're not going to give me *that* old line, are you?"

"It's true," he said defensively, looking at her from over the rim of his coffee cup. "This is a man's place, Ashley." He was about to say more, but was interrupted by the slamming of a door. He looked up just as his assistant hurled a set of car keys at the wall.

"Women!" the man roared, oblivious to his small audience. His stride was long and powerful, his shoulders sweeping. "Who can understand them?" He skidded to a halt when he saw Ashley. "Uh, sorry, Jeeter. I didn't know you had company."

Jeeter didn't seem the least bit perturbed as he motioned the man over. "Jack, this is my niece, Ashley Rogers. You've heard me talk about her. Ashley, meet Jack Sloan."

Jack stood motionless for a minute while taking in the woman before him. He tried to recall the things Jeeter had said about her. For the life of him, he couldn't remember. Except that she was a librarian or something he considered equally dull. He'd expected a short, pudgy woman with thick glasses and a sour face. She didn't look like any librarian he'd ever met. He closed the distance between them, wiped his hand on his jeans, and held it out. The woman smiled and shook it. Her hand fit nicely into his.

"Uh, hello," he said.

His grip was strong, Ashley noted. His palm felt like toughened rawhide, a direct contrast to the masculine beauty of his hand and the long, tapering fingers with neatly trimmed nails.

"Nice to meet you, Mr. Sloan," she said. He nodded in return, and the motion of his head drew her attention to the thick coffee-colored hair that curled well past his collar, giving him a wild, almost reckless appearance. It was too long to be stylish, she noted, but flattering enough to catch any woman's eye.

Jack regarded the woman before him with a practiced, critical eye. "Same here," he mumbled distractedly. He released her hand with a great deal of reluctance. For a moment he wanted to shake Jeeter. The man had obviously left out a few pertinent details about his niece.

"I've heard a great deal about you," Ashley said. "It's funny we've never met."

Jack nodded dumbly. He still couldn't believe this was Jeeter Hamil's niece. Not that Jeeter wasn't an okay guy, but he was a bit sloppy at times, what with his tobacco chewing and cigar smoking. And he couldn't remember the last time Jeeter had washed his coffee cup. This woman appeared to be nothing like her uncle. Her long dark hair was squeaky clean and shiny. She wore very little makeup, but there was a radiance about her, a sparkle, that had nothing to do with cosmetics.

"Ashley quit her job at the library," Jeeter said, looking from one to the other.

"Congratulations," Jack said, one corner of his mouth turning upward into a smile. He couldn't imagine a woman like her spending her life among a bunch of musty old books.

His response surprised Ashley. Why would a person offer congratulations to someone who had just become unemployed? She raised her eyes to the man before her, and their gazes locked. Her mouth went dry. She felt unusually warm, as though the thermostat had just been turned up thirty degrees. Suddenly, the air around her seemed insufficient. His gaze dropped from her eyes to her mouth, and she felt as though he'd physically traced it with his fingertips. Her lips felt parched, and she moistened them with the tip of her tongue.

Jack didn't miss the movement. An unexpected surge of desire filled his lower belly, and surprised him as much as it pleased him. His eyes were hypnotically drawn to her lips. That pink tongue had rattled him. It made him think of things that should be kept in the privacy of the bedroom.

If Jeeter noticed the sudden, almost tangible air of electricity between the two, he didn't mention it. "So what happened on the Adams case?" he asked his assistant.

"Huh?" The question drew a blank look from Jack. He reeled in his thoughts and felt some of his old irritation return. "Jeeter, that woman is a raving lunatic!"

Jeeter chuckled, and his shoulders shook slightly with the effort. "What did she do this time?"

Jack planted his hands on his hips and shook his head as though totally exasperated. He glanced at Ashley and saw that she was listening as well, a smile teasing the corners of her full lips. "Mrs. Adams had to see for herself that her husband was cheating on her, so I took her by the apartment building where her husband's . . . uh, lady friend lives, and we waited for him to show up." He glanced at Ashley once more. "These two meet every day at lunch to grab a little afternoon delight."

Ashley smiled and nodded. "I think I get the picture."

"Anyway, Mr. Adams pulls up in his car and goes inside the building—" Jack paused, covering his eyes. "Lord, I still can't believe it. Mrs. Adams slams out of the car and runs into the building like a madwoman. I thought she was going to rip the door off its hinges. By the time I got inside, she was already in the apartment, clawing her husband's eyes out. Naturally, his girlfriend called the police. I swear, Jeeter, I couldn't get the woman out of there. She was throwing things and turning over furniture as if she were in a regular demolition derby."

"What did the police do?"

"They locked her up," he answered matter-of-factly. "And I had to bail her out, because her husband was too scared to do it himself." Jack shook his head, crossed the room to his desk, and slumped into his chair while the other two laughed. He reached into his pocket, drew out a crushed pack of cigarettes, and lighted one. He snapped his old metal lighter closed and pocketed it once more.

Jeeter was still laughing when he spoke. "Jack has been with me for two years now," he told Ashley. "He used to be a cop. Best detective I've ever had. Makes Magnum P.I. look like a sissy."

With the cigarette anchored between his square, even teeth, Jack mumbled something and opened a telephone book. He scanned the listings. He had no idea what he was looking for, but it beat the hell out of staring at Jeeter's niece. He tried once again to remember what Jeeter had told him about her, and silently cursed the fact that he hadn't paid closer attention. But then, Jeeter had a habit of rambling, and Jack had learned long ago to block out about half of what the man said. He thought he remembered something about her having children, but he had no idea how many. She was either widowed or divorced, because Jeeter had offered to fix them up once, a suggestion that Jack had turned down flat. Now, he could kick himself.

"Ashley here wants to become a private detective," Jeeter said. "What d'you think of that?"

Jack looked up and found himself staring into those same blue eyes again. Teal blue. He'd spotted the color recently on a brand-new Mercedes and had inquired about it. The car had been specially ordered by the owner, and Jack had thought it was the prettiest color he'd ever seen.

"That's nice," he said, noting that Jeeter was expecting some sort of reply.

"She wants to come to work here," Jeeter added.

Jack was jolted from his thoughts. "Here?" He looked from one to the other, thinking perhaps Jeeter was pulling his leg. Both looked serious. He tried to swallow, but there wasn't a drop of spit left in his mouth. *"Here?"* he repeated dumbly, emphasizing the word this time. Jeeter nodded.

Ashley did not miss the look of utter disbelief on Jack's face, and decided it was time she did her own talking. "Mr. Sloan, I'm a hard worker. And I learn fast. I know I could do the job. It's something I've always secretly yearned to do." She was rambling and she knew it, but his face was growing more doubtful by the minute. "I read every detective magazine I can get my hands on." Ashley mentally chided herself for that last remark. Reading detective magazines didn't exactly qualify her for the job.

Jack didn't know how to respond. He hated to inform her flat out that she was wasting her time. That was Jeeter's role. Instead, he leaned back in his chair and propped his feet on the top of his desk and waited, while the silence stretched out between them. Jeeter would never hire her. For one thing, she was inexperienced. Second, she was a woman. Jeeter would never hire someone without experience, relative or not, and he would never, ever hire a woman for what he considered a man's job. Now, all he had to do was break it to his niece gently.

"What d'you say we give her a try, Jack?" Jeeter said after a moment.

Jack almost tipped over in his chair. His feet came down hard on the floor as he tried to balance himself and prevent a nasty spill. "You're not serious?"

Jeeter winked at him, which went unnoticed by his niece. "Let's give her a week and see what she can do. If it doesn't work out, then neither of us holds a grudge."

Jack had difficulty finding his tongue. "But she has no experience, Jeeter."

"Neither did I when I started."

"And she doesn't have a license."

Jeeter waved the technicality aside. "I got friends in high places, boy. If I can pull a few strings and get her in front of the board this afternoon, I can have her approved by suppertime. It worked for you, didn't it?"

Jack didn't believe his own ears. "But she . . . she could get shot messing around in the wrong place at the wrong time. She doesn't know the first thing about protecting herself." He raked his fingers through his hair. What could Jeeter be thinking?

"She won't get shot if she's with you," Jeeter replied evenly. "One week, Jack."

Jack temporarily lost his place in the conversation when Ashley smiled brightly at her uncle. One cheek puckered near the corner of her mouth into a tiny dimple that looked quite kissable. "I can't believe you'd even consider it, Jeeter," he said. "Besides, you know I work alone."

"Mr. Sloan, I promise to stay out of your way," Ashley said dutifully, pleased but a little apprehensive about having to work so closely with Jack. She hoped she could keep her mind on her work.

Jack wasn't listening. Had the whole world gone mad? Jeeter didn't know what he was doing. He was letting his emotions get in the way of his judgment, and it was up to Jack to make him see that. "Jeeter, may I speak to you in private?"

Jeeter nodded. "Let's go out into the hall." He stood and hiked his pants up over his belly. "We'll be right back, sugar," he told Ashley, and patted her on the shoulder.

Once they were alone, Jack didn't hesitate to give Jeeter his opinion. "Have you lost your mind?"

"She needs a job, Jack."

"Not here, she doesn't."

"She's been turned down all over town. Her confidence is shot to hell."

"Then let her type or answer the phone."

"She's not interested in doing office work. She wants to do something else with her life. She has a family to support. This could be her break into a good career. Once you show her the ropes, I could put her on surveillance work. That's safe enough."

"I don't want to be responsible for her, Jeeter," Jack stated flatly.

"Aw, so now we're getting down to the real reason behind this," the man answered knowingly. "I'm supposed to turn her down because you have some kind of hang-up about taking charge?"

Jack felt as though Jeeter had just punched him in the gut. For a moment all he could do was stare at the man. So Jeeter was going to fight dirty, eh? "I told you from the beginning how it was."

"Yeah, but I'd hoped you'd changed. The business is growing, thanks to you, so it's no surprise that we'll need new people from time to time. I want you to train those people." He slung his arm over the younger man's shoulder. "This may be good for you, Jack. Just the thing you need. Besides, you can't spend the rest of your life blaming yourself for what happened to those men."

"I was their superior officer."

Jeeter went on as though he hadn't heard. "And there's nobody else in the world I would trust with my niece's safety."

Jack was feeling desperate. "Jeeter, for heaven's sake—"

"You're a leader, Jack. You could turn this outfit into a big-time operation."

"That's not what I want."

"Are you sure?" When Jack didn't answer right away, Jeeter went on, "Are you content to work for some Podunk agency for the rest of your life? Are you willing to waste what God-given talents you have just because of a little bad luck?"

Jack's face flamed. "How can you refer to ruthless murdering as just a little bad luck?" he flung back at the man.

Jeeter sighed and dropped his arm from Jack's shoulder. "I want you to do this for me, Jack. Give Ashley a chance. Hopefully, you'll be offering yourself another chance as well. That's what life is all about—giving and taking chances. What d'you say?"

Ashley twisted her fingers in her lap. Her uncle wasn't going to hire her. He was only trying to think of a polite way to turn her down. She shouldn't have come in the first place, she told herself, no matter how desperately she needed the job. She had put Uncle Jeeter on the spot in front of his brown-eyed assistant, who looked like a refugee from the Woodstock festival in his worn denims and tie-dyed T-shirt that clung to his broad chest like a second skin. It showed off his finely muscled arms, the taut biceps.

He epitomized male sensuality with those dark, hooded eyes and daredevil looks.

Ashley glanced at the door through which they'd disappeared. She would make it easy on both of them, and say she'd changed her mind. She stood and turned for the door just as her uncle walked through with Jack on his heels.

"You can start tomorrow," Jeeter said, wearing a big grin.

Shock rendered her speechless for a moment. "I can?" Her gaze wandered to Jack. His face was unreadable.

Jeeter gave her a bone-crushing hug. "I'll get on the phone right away and see what I can do about getting you a temporary license. Are you free for the day?"

She nodded dumbly. "Chip is watching Mikie."

"Well, there's a million and one things to do, if you want to start right away."

"Of course. Whatever it takes." She still couldn't believe she had the job.

"Meet me here tomorrow morning at seven o'clock sharp," said Jack, already regretting that he'd agreed to train her. He wouldn't get a damn thing accomplished with her tagging along.

Ashley could see from the look on his face, he wasn't happy with her uncle's decision to hire her. He didn't want her there, but that only made her more determined to do her best. "Thanks, Mr. Sloan," she said, offering her hand. "I promise, you won't regret this."

Jack stared at her hand for several seconds before he took it in his own. He was surprised again by how dainty it was. "Welcome aboard," he said, mustering up the closest thing he could to a smile. Inside, he could feel his doubts churning and eating at the pit of his stomach like an ulcer.

Ashley arrived home hot and exhausted. She found her sixteen-year-old son, Chip, waiting to take his younger brother to T-ball practice. "How'd it go?" he asked Ashley as she tossed him the keys to the car.

She smiled tiredly. "I got the job."

He beamed. "Good for you. When do you start?"

"Tomorrow. I spent the entire day filling out forms so I could get a temporary license. I had no idea it was so involved."

"I knew you could do it, Mom."

Ashley watched them pull away in her car. She couldn't begin to think what she'd do without Chip. Besides working nights and weekends in a local supermarket, he was a tremendous help with his brother. It wasn't fair, she told herself. Chip had never had much of a childhood. He'd been forced to grow up quickly in the four years since his father had been gone. Chip was nothing like his father. Her son was levelheaded and dependable, traits she had never found in her ex-husband.

Ashley pulled a package of ground beef from the refrigerator and shaped it into hamburger patties as she went over in her mind the events of the day. It was sheer luck that her uncle was able to get her the temporary license, and something she felt sure didn't happen often. Hadn't she been told that very thing several times by the people who'd approved her? Good ol' Uncle Jeeter. He'd come through for her when she really needed him. She hoped to return the favor by doing a great job for him.

Ashley had just placed the hamburger patties on a broiler pan when she heard a motorcycle out front. Thinking it must be one of Chip's friends, she shot a casual glance out the window, and was surprised by the enormous size of the bike as well as the man riding it. He was definitely not one of Chip's friends.

Still peering out the window, Ashley watched the man climb from the bike and make his way across the yard to the front door, unsnapping his helmet with one hand. Although he looked vaguely familiar, Ashley couldn't place him. A second later, the doorbell rang, and she hurried to answer it. She opened the door and found herself looking into the face of Jack Sloan. Her heart rate went into double-time.

"Jeeter gave me your address," he said without preamble. The lady was more than a little surprised to see him, he noted. "I need a favor." He felt guilty as hell asking her to do something for him after the argument he'd put up about hiring her.

"Yes?"

"Would you mind piercing my left ear?"

Ashley cocked her head to the side, thinking she had misunderstood him. "You want me to pierce your ear?" she repeated mechanically.

"Yeah. Can I come in? It's like an oven out here."

"Oh, yes, please do." Ashley held the door open wide enough for him to pass through. He paused on the threshold and glanced around the room expectantly.

"Something wrong?"

"I thought you had kids."

"I do. They're not here right now."

"Boys or girls?"

"Two boys. Five and sixteen."

"Lady, you don't look old enough to have a sixteen-year-old, and I'm not saying that just to make you feel good." His gaze dropped to her shoes, then very slowly climbed the length of her.

"Well, thank you," she said, feeling warm and flushed after his very blatant perusal. "I married young, and started my family right away." Ashley tried not to notice how rugged and untamed he looked in a pair of indecently tight jeans and a form-fitting knit shirt. The V at his neck displayed a nest of dark hair, and just looking at it made her acutely aware of the rest of his body.

"Would you like something cold to drink?" she asked.

"Yeah, a scotch and water would be nice."

"I was about to suggest a glass of iced tea," she said. "I'm afraid I don't have any, uh, alcohol in the house." She fidgeted with her hands. "Not that I'm opposed to it or anything like that, it's just I never think to buy it and—"

"Tea will be fine."

Ashley nodded and closed the front door, then led him into the kitchen, where she opened the refrigerator and pulled out a tall pitcher of tea. She motioned for Jack to take a seat at the kitchen table while she poured the tea into two tall glasses. "Now what's this about piercing your ear?" she said, once she'd taken a seat across the table from him.

He didn't hesitate. "I'm working on this case," he began, "which involves a motorcycle gang." When he saw the shocked expression on her face, he chuckled. "It's not as bad as it sounds. They're really not bad people."

"I'll take your word for it."

"Anyway, I've been out partying with them a few times in order to win their confidence, and every time they have a few beers under their belts, they want to pierce my ear. I think it's part of their initiation or something, but all the guys in the group have a pierced left ear."

"If they've already offered to do it, then why are you asking me?"

He shifted in his chair. "Because they'll probably pierce it with a dirty pocket knife or something, and I don't want to risk an infection. I want it done right." He paused briefly. "I thought about going to one of those jewelry stores at the mall, but I'd feel like a fool standing in line with a bunch of teenage girls. Jeeter suggested I come to you."

She looked skeptical. "Are you sure about this?"

"I've never been more sure of anything in my life."

"Okay, I'll do it," she finally agreed.

He looked relieved. "I'm supposed to meet them at a bar tonight."

Ashley took a sip of her iced tea. "What's the case about?" she asked. "That is, if you can discuss it."

He shrugged. "A man who disappeared five years ago is suspected of being a member of this group. All this time his family has thought him dead, but recently someone claimed to have spotted the guy with this motorcycle gang."

"Is he married?"

"Married with three kids."

She looked surprised. "And he just up and left?" At Jack's nod, her look hardened. "Then I hope you catch the worm." He grinned at her response, and she thought it made him look younger.

"One of the first rules in this business is not to

get personally involved on a case," he said, then drained his tea in one gulp.

"You're certain this gang is safe?" For some reason she was concerned about him. He appeared to be the type who took unnecessary chances—but then, that was part of his appeal.

"I'm safe as long as I don't let them near my ears. Of course, there's a problem with the women," he added. "They've complained several times that I'm not . . . uh, friendly. But I don't want to get involved with any of the ladies in that group, if you know what I mean."

"Why don't you take a date, so you won't have that problem?"

He gave her a funny look. "Ask someone to accompany me to a party with a bunch of bikers?" He laughed. "How about you? Would you like to take time out from playing Donna Reed and go?"

"You don't have to be sarcastic."

"I wasn't trying to be. I just don't understand why a woman like you would be remotely interested in detective work." He wondered briefly if perhaps he *should* let her in on the case. The gang was loud and dirty and downright indecent at times. He forced back the grin that threatened to break out on his face as he tried to imagine Jeeter's niece getting to know the bikers' women. She would flip. And probably change her mind about working for the agency.

That wasn't a bad idea.

"I told you, I've always been fascinated with that kind of work." She sighed. How would she ever make him understand? she wondered. How many times had she sat in the ghostly silence of the library and longed for a more challenging career? Something she could sink her teeth into. Finding her uncle's advertisement for help in the classifieds had been the answer to her prayers. All she had to do was convince him she could do the job. Now, she had to convince Jack.

Ashley decided it was time to change the subject. She was not going to persuade Jack overnight. Perhaps if he got to know her better, saw how determined she was to do well . . . It suddenly was very important to her that she prove herself to this man. "Would you like to stay for dinner?" she blurted out before taking the time to think.

Jack was surprised at the invitation, but prepared to turn her down, nevertheless. He pondered the idea. He really wasn't in a hurry to leave, for some reason, although he suspected it would be quite an experience sharing a meal with her boys. What would they think of him? He wasn't exactly dressed for the occasion. But he liked talking to Ashley. She seemed genuinely interested in what he had to say. Most women seemed to prefer talking about themselves. "Yeah, thanks," he finally answered. "I'd like that."

Ashley was pleased and a bit surprised that Jack had agreed to stay. She couldn't imagine how her boys would react to him, though, and that thought bothered her a little. "It will be nice having another adult at the dinner table," she heard herself say.

"Now, about piercing my ear . . ."

She stood. "I'll pierce it just as soon as I get the hamburgers under the broiler." She hurried to the refrigerator and opened the freezer door. "In the meantime you can numb your ear with an ice cube." She brought out an ice tray, took a cube from it, and wrapped it in a paper towel. "Just hold it against your ear, like this," she said, showing him where to put it. Her knuckles brushed against his jawbone, and she stepped away quickly.

If Jack noticed, he gave no indication. He merely took the ice from her and placed it against his earlobe. "Are you sure this will numb it?" he asked.

She nodded distractedly, wondering why she was so skittish around him. "It worked for me." She went back to preparing dinner.

Ten minutes later, Ashley stood before Jack holding a potato and a sterilized sewing needle. She had also sterilized the single loop earring he'd given her.

Jack visibly tensed. "Wait a minute," he said, holding her off. "What are you going to do with that potato? And don't you think that needle is too large for the job?"

"Just relax and hold still. All you're going to feel is a little prick." Jack's back and shoulders were rigid as Ashley anchored the potato behind his ear. She stuck the needle through in one fluid motion.

Jack's shoulders sagged in relief. "Hey, that wasn't so bad after all." But getting the earring through the tiny hole was another matter. Jack grew paler each time she tried. After several attempts, Ashley finally accomplished it, then cleaned the earlobe with rubbing alcohol and dabbed it with bacitracin. She warned him to repeat the cleaning procedure morning and night for the next ten days.

"Thanks," he said, once he'd looked into the hand mirror she gave him. The earring was centered perfectly in the earlobe. He was glad that he'd asked her to do it. He knew several ladies who could have pierced his ear for him, but he hadn't trusted any of them as much as he'd trusted Ashley. Odd thing was, he barely knew her. Still, there was something about her that inspired confidence. He glanced back at his reflection. He only hoped the hole would grow back together once he finished the case.

Ashley checked on the hamburgers and turned them over before sliding the broiler pan back into the oven. "Did you say Uncle Jeeter told you how to get here?" she asked over her shoulder.

Jack nodded. "Jeeter's an okay guy," he said, suddenly realizing he was staring at her. She'd pinned up her long hair, exposing gracefully sloping shoulders. Her waist was slim, her hips gently flared, and she had the prettiest legs he'd ever seen, trim ankles and shapely calves that made his mouth water. He would definitely turn into a leg man if he spent much time with her. Jeeter had told him her husband had run out on her and the kids before the youngest had celebrated his first birthday.

Jack's old man had walked out when he'd been just a kid, and he knew firsthand how a father's departure tore the guts out of a family. He was thankful there had been no children born of his own brief marriage. He'd never known what it was like to grow up feeling loved and secure. He'd been forced to grow up fast. Continuing his education had been out of the question, since he'd had to work full time, but knowing how to find the square root of a number hadn't seemed as important as keeping food in his brothers' bellies. He had a soft spot for kids. He didn't like to think of them going cold or hungry or being abused. He wasn't wealthy by any means, but he made a habit of dropping money into those containers they kept on the counters in some convenience stores. Those sad-eyed children haunted him.

He knew what it was like to do without. Still, Jack couldn't imagine a man walking away from a woman who looked like Ashley.

Ashley could feel Jack's gaze on her as she opened a cabinet door and pulled out four dinner plates. She carried them to the table and placed each one beside a set of silverware. She felt very self-conscious. She should say something, she told herself, but every time she looked at him, her thoughts scattered like breeze-ridden dandelion fluff.

"You have a nice home," Jack said, feeling the need to break the silence.

Ashley was pleased with the compliment. "Thank you. My son and I recently painted the interior. We're thinking about painting the outside this summer. In fact, I already have the paint."

"That's a lot of work."

"Yes, but it needs it. The color has faded." Why did she feel she had to make excuses about her house to the man? she wondered, taking a head of lettuce from the refrigerator. Because the house had needed a lot of work, she had bought it at a good price after her divorce. She had decorated it inexpensively, most of the furnishings purchased from garage sales and secondhand stores. She had repainted and stenciled designs on some walls and furniture to give them a custom look. After having taken an upholstering course at the community college, she'd single-handedly upholstered her sofa and chair with fabric from an interior-decorating store that had been discontinued and suitably marked down. It didn't look like the showroom at Macy's, but she could live with it, and it was even more special because she'd done it by herself. Her friends thought she was clever, painting and covering her own furniture or being able to whip up a new dress for herself or a shirt for her boys on her sewing machine. She was thankful for the ability—it certainly helped her out of tight spots when she needed something, but she wondered sometimes what it would be like to walk into a store like Saks and buy right off the rack.

Ashley glanced at the hamburgers and saw they were ready, then remembered the French fries. It wasn't easy preparing dinner under Jack's watchful gaze, she admitted to herself. She grabbed a bag of frozen French fries from the freezer and placed them on a cookie sheet. While they baked, she prepared a big salad, all the while trying to keep up her end of the conversation. She was almost thankful when she heard Chip pull up in the driveway.

"Dinner is ready," she announced, as her oldest walked through the front door with his brother behind him.

Chip didn't seem the least bit interested. "Whose bike is that outside?" he asked, hurrying into the kitchen. "It's awesome!" He saw Jack and skidded to a halt. His younger brother slammed into him. Their eyes grew as large as saucers when they spotted Jack.

"This is Mr. Sloan," Ashley told them. "He works with Uncle Jeeter." When nobody said anything, she went on, "Jack, meet my sons, Chip and Mikie."

"Is that your bike?" Chip asked, once he'd regained his composure.

Jack nodded. "And the name's Jack. Not Mr. Sloan."

The boys stared back at Jack with uncertainty,

now that they were over their initial excitement. They looked at their mother as if waiting for an explanation.

"Why is he here?" Mikie asked when Ashley didn't supply the information right away.

Ashley felt the heat rush to her cheeks at her son's tactless question. "I invited him to dinner, that's why. He and I will be working together at Uncle Jeeter's agency," she added, hoping to impress them, but the boys merely continued to stare at Jack as though he'd just fallen off some other planet. It was obvious their mother didn't make a habit of bringing home strange men.

Jack shifted in his chair. He felt like an insect under a microscope. "Nice to meet you," he said.

"He has long hair," Mikie pointed out, to everyone's surprise. "And he's wearing an earring."

"Your mother pierced my ear," Jack informed him, laying a finger tentatively against the small golden loop.

Chip looked at his mother in disbelief. "You pierced his ear?"

"I wouldn't want to have a hole in my ear," Mikie said, cupping his ears with his palms as though someone were after him with a needle.

"Could we please change the subject?" Ashley asked. "And while you're at it, wash your hands for dinner." Chip gave her a long, searching look before he left the room. While the boys washed up in the guest bathroom, Ashley set the food on the table, carefully avoiding Jack's gaze. It had been a mistake to invite him, she fretted.

Dinner was a strained affair, and Ashley was glad when it was over. The boys carried their plates to the sink, and disappeared into the living room to watch TV.

"I'm sorry Chip and Mikie picked you apart over dinner," Ashley said.

Jack waved the statement aside, but at the same time he was glad for the reprieve. "Forget it."

"They're very outspoken at times, but they don't mean to be rude. Would you like a cup of coffee?"

Jack glanced at his watch. "Yeah, and then I have to go."

Ashley loaded the dishwasher and made small talk while she waited for the coffee to drip through the coffee maker.

"So you used to be a policeman," she said, once she'd sat down. He looked anything but. "Why did you give it up?" Jack's jaw hardened perceptibly, and Ashley regretted the question and wished she could take it back.

"Cops are getting their heads blown off every day. It wasn't worth the risk." He paused and lighted a cigarette. "Has anybody ever told you you have nice hair?"

The abrupt change of subject caught Ashley by surprise. "Uh, thanks." She jumped from the table and searched one of the kitchen cabinets for an ashtray. He thanked her when she rejoined him at the table. Her gaze wandered over his face as he smoked silently for a moment. He really was nice-looking, in a wild sort of way, even with his longer hair. It was clean and shiny and healthy looking. And although his jeans were faded and almost threadbare at the knees, they looked clean as well—and very sexy.

Jack stubbed out the cigarette and stood. "I have to go now."

Ashley got to her feet once more. "I suppose you have to meet the infamous motorcycle gang," she said matter-of-factly. "It sounds a bit exciting, if you ask me."

"You're free to come with me," he responded, cocking his head to the side. His eyes challenged her.

She tilted her head back, raising her chin defiantly. "I'm not afraid to go."

He made his way to the front door with her on his heels. "You're not dressed for the part. Maybe next time, Sherlock."

He was making fun of her, Ashley told herself. He didn't think she had the guts for the job. "I could change."

Jack chuckled under his breath as he let himself out the front door and headed for his bike, leaving her standing on the front steps wearing a dejected frown. He probably should forget his original idea to let her come along, he thought. It wasn't dangerous, but it would probably scare the daylights out of her. He brought himself up short. If she wanted him to train her, she had to be prepared for what he dished out. He couldn't let the fact that she was a woman—a beautiful woman—interfere with their work.

He turned slowly, and when he looked at her, his expression was almost smug. "Yeah, why don't you? Change clothes, that is. I could probably use your help after all."

Her mouth fell open, forming a big O. She closed it. "You really want me to go with you?" she asked after a moment.

"If you think you know how to act," he answered,

stuffing his hands in the pockets of his jeans, which was no small task, considering how tight they were. He rocked back and forth on the heel of his boots, studying her with a critical eye. "I trust you won't start pulling out snapshots of your kids or try to swap recipes with the bikers' women." He almost smiled as she pressed her lips together in irritation.

"I'm not entirely dim-witted," she said.

"Then it's up to you." She won't go, he told himself. And it was just as well, because she'd probably blow their cover. But frankly, he would have derived some satisfaction out of showing her that private investigative work wasn't as fun as they made it look on TV.

He didn't think she'd do it, Ashley told herself, reading the arrogant look on his face. "Give me five minutes," she said. She raced inside the house and to her bedroom, missing his look of surprise.

Two

Chip glanced up from the television set as his mother hurried into her bedroom. He followed. "What's going on?" he asked, stopping just inside the door.

Ashley pulled a pair of tattered jeans from a dresser drawer and faced him. "I'm going on my first assignment," she said breathlessly. She was both nervous and excited, but determined to do a good job and win Jack's vote of confidence. She opened several other drawers in search of an old shirt.

"You're going to wear *that* on an assignment?" Chip motioned to her clothes in disbelief. "Just what kind of assignment is it?"

"I don't think I'm supposed to talk about it," she said. "But don't worry, it's nothing dangerous." She hoped. Lord, what was she getting herself into? She had two children to care for. But she wanted a new career, right? Something she could build on. Besides, people weren't exactly banging at her front door with job offers. The fact that Jack Sloan wasn't crazy about her coming to work for her uncle's agency was only a temporary deterrent. She would show him. The thought made her heart flutter.

"Mom, I don't like all this secrecy," Chip said. "When you said you were going to go to work for Uncle Jeeter, I thought you were going to do his typing. I never suspected you'd be going off with some . . . hood."

"Please stop worrying, Chip," she said, placing an open palm against his cheek. He was too young to shoulder so many worries, she thought. "Now run along so I can get dressed, and please don't call Mr. Sloan a hood to his face."

Five minutes later, after giving instructions to her skeptical son, Ashley hurried out the front door. She found Jack waiting on the front steps. He did a double-take when he saw her. A slow grin drew the corners of his mouth upward.

"Hey, that's more like it," he said, his deep voice rumbling with appreciation. The denims were tight, emphasizing her long legs. And when she turned to lock the front door, he almost fell down the steps. She had the cutest tush he'd ever laid eyes on. Her shirttail, which had been tied at the waist, drew the cotton material tight across her breasts and emphasized the swell of her hips. "I like it when you don't dress like a librarian."

Ashley didn't know quite how to respond. His blatant look sent a small shiver down her spine. "Uh, thanks," she managed, but her knees felt weak as she descended the front steps. He climbed onto his motorcycle and patted the seat behind him. Ashley stopped in her tracks.

"We're . . . uh . . . riding that?" she asked hesitantly. She was thankful the boys were inside.

Jack saw the worry in her eyes. So she was scared of motorcycles. Perfect. "What else would you ride to a bikers' party?"

"But I'm—" She had been about to confess her fear of motorcycles, but thought better of it. Jack would gloat for the rest of his life. Instead, she gritted her teeth, pulled on a helmet, climbed on the bike, and forced herself to smile.

Jack swallowed the chuckle that threatened to escape his throat. "Slide your butt forward and put your arms around my waist," he told her. Ashley rolled her eyes heavenward, convincing herself she'd never be able to do it, but she scooted forward nevertheless and put her arms around him. A hot blush scalded her cheeks as she came in contact with the hard muscles of his stomach, but she clung to him tightly out of fear, her breasts flattened against his wide back. His after-shave filled the air she breathed and made her stomach feel funny, like the gooey insides of a roasted marshmallow. Jack put the motorcycle into gear and whizzed down the street, while curious neighbors peered from their windows. Ashley buried her face in his shoulder and hung on for dear life.

"You can loosen your death grip on me," Jack told her a few minutes later. "You're not going to fall." Ashley didn't budge. "People aren't going to believe you're a biker's woman if you act terrified of motorcycles." Actually, she felt pretty damn good pressed against him, and he could feel his body responding to her nearness.

Slowly, Ashley lifted her head, but she didn't release her grip on his waist. "How fast are we going?" she asked breathlessly.

He grinned. "Twenty miles per hour. We're still in a residential area. Are you sure you want in on this case?"

She nodded and loosened her hold on him. She took a deep breath. "I'm okay now," she said, trying to convince herself as well as him.

The Roadhouse Bar was located in the middle of nowhere, Ashley discovered. However, it didn't look as though it was hurting for business. At least a dozen or more motorcycles were parked out front, as well as a sizable number of cars. Jack parked his bike, cut off the engine, and laid the ground rules as he strapped their helmets to the seat.

"Let me do all the talking," he said. "If somebody asks you something, think twice before you answer, and remember, don't give out your real name to anybody."

She nodded stiffly, a grim look on her face. She could do it. She'd show Jack Sloan she wasn't made of fluff.

"And relax. These people like to party. They probably won't even know you're in the room." He seriously doubted it, but it seemed to make her feel better. She was putting up a good front, and he admired her for that, even if it wasn't what he'd planned. "Oh, I almost forgot the reason we came," he said, pulling out his wallet. He opened it and flipped through several pictures before he pulled out a worn photograph. "This is the man we're looking for," he told her. "He's about forty years old, and could be wearing a beard. If you see him, don't say or do anything, just tell me."

Ashley studied the picture briefly before handing it back to Jack. "You mean he just disappeared off the face of the earth?"

Jack nodded, folded the wallet, and stuffed it in his back pocket. "Ready?" he asked once they'd made it to the front door. When Ashley nodded, he pushed it open and motioned for her to step through.

Ashley blinked several times as her eyes tried to adjust to the dim light inside the building. When she was finally able to see clearly, she stifled the urge to turn around and run right back out the door. Seated in several groups before her were at least twenty bikers and their women.

"Over here, Spike," one of the men called from the back of the group, and motioned them over. Jack guided Ashley toward the table, using his hand at the small of her back. Oddly enough, it felt warm and comforting.

"Remember," he said, leaning forward to whisper in her ear, "let me do all the talking." She nodded.

"Where'd you get the good-looking broad?" the biker asked as Jack grabbed a couple of chairs and dragged them to the table.

Ashley, aware that several pairs of eyes were trained on her, merely smiled as Jack made the introductions. "This is Angel," he said, slinging an arm around her possessively. He pulled her close, tucking her head under his chin.

Ashley nodded at the group, but her thoughts suddenly shifted to Jack, making her less tense. The scent of his after-shave was even stronger, tangier. The stubble of his beard scratched her forehead, but felt nice just the same. His breath was warm and pleasant, and each time he spoke, she could feel the words rumbling in his chest. It wasn't a bad place to be, she decided. She felt safe and protected, a feeling that was as new to her as spending her evening with a bunch of bikers.

"Where'd you find this little jewel?" another man questioned.

Jack didn't hesitate. "She used to be married to a biker friend of mine," he replied casually. "But he split for California a few years back. Left her high and dry."

"Hey, bummer," the man answered, giving Ashley a sympathetic look. "I can't imagine any man walking out on that sweet thing."

"I know what you mean," Jack said, winking at the man. Inside, he was a bit edgy. It didn't take a genius to notice that the room had suddenly become quieter or that some of the men were looking at Ashley. She had to wear those butt-grabbing jeans, he thought. If one of them so much as laid a hand on her . . . He hadn't considered that possibility, but now he realized he might have jeopardized Ashley's safety by bringing her. Talk about unprofessional! What if one of the guys *did* put the moves on her? He'd have to punch him out, or at least try to, and that would blow everything. He was going to have to stick to her like rubber cement. He pulled a chair out for Ashley and took one for himself, then motioned for a waitress. "Can we get a couple of drafts over here?" The woman standing behind the bar nodded.

Ashley was aware of the rather blatant stares a couple of the men were giving her. Jack's hand slipped beneath the table and squeezed her knee reassuringly. It worked. She felt the tension seep from her body.

Ashley suddenly remembered why they were there, and she scanned the faces around her. None of them resembled the face in the photograph Jack had shown her, but it was difficult to tell, since many of the bikers had facial hair. She couldn't help but notice in her perusal that all of them had a pierced left ear as Jack had said, and some of them wore up to six earrings in one earlobe. As though reading her thoughts, a biker at the center table noticed Jack's earring and brought it to the attention of the others. Jack beamed proudly at Ashley.

She couldn't help but smile back. He really was good-looking, she thought to herself, wondering if it was that wild, devil-may-care look and attitude that attracted her. Not to mention those skintight jeans he wore. He was nothing like the men she dated occasionally, who dressed neatly in gabardine slacks and oxford shirts and had normal office jobs and took her to places like Morrison's and Pizza Hut. If any of them had suggested she hop on a motorcycle and go partying with a bunch of bikers, she'd have laughed them out of the room.

"Hey, I got a great idea," a man named Trooper said. "Let's buy some beer and go skinny-dipping at the lake. We still got a couple of hours of daylight."

The group cheered his idea. Ashley raised her eyes to Jack's in a what-do-we-do-now look. He smiled and whispered, "We don't have to go if you don't want to."

"Hey, Spike, you're bringing Angel, aren't you?" a biker named Kojack asked. "The two of you have to meet our friends at the lake. Real cool dudes." Before Jack could answer, the same man appealed to Ashley. "You want to go, Angel, don't you?"

It was the first time Ashley spoke. "Well, I—"

"Sure you do," he interrupted. "Come on, you two." He motioned for them to follow as he left the table with the rest of the group and slung his arm around a woman.

"Now what?" Ashley whispered frantically to Jack. Surely, he wouldn't go along with the plan? No matter how badly she wanted to impress him, she couldn't imagine herself swimming buck-naked with a group that resembled Hell's Angels.

The color had drained from Jack's face. "We'll follow them to the store for beer, then come up with an excuse to leave," he said.

"But what if one of the people at the lake house happens to be the man you're looking for?"

He pondered it. "Okay, we'll go as far as the lake, *then* beg off."

"Don't you think they're going to be suspicious? What if it destroys the trust you've worked so hard to build?"

"Would you stop firing questions at me?" Jack said, prodding her forward as the group emptied out the front door of the bar. "You should have been prepared for something like this. This job is full of surprises." Actually, though, he didn't like the thought of her stripping down any better than she did, and he was just taking out his anger at himself on her. It was his own fault for bringing her. He only hoped Ashley was beginning to realize what she had got them both into.

Jack climbed on his motorcycle, then motioned for her to get on. A chorus of motorcycle engines roared loudly before the group shot onto the highway one by one. Jack and Ashley were among the last to take off.

I don't believe this is happening to me, Ashley thought, as the throng of bikers sped along the road in groups of two. She couldn't help but notice the stares of those motorists driving in the opposite direction. Lord, please return me safely to my children, she prayed, and I promise I'll never get on another motorcycle for as long as I live. She was thankful when they pulled up in front of a convenience store. Several women climbed from their bikes and began collecting money.

"Are you okay?" Jack whispered, once he'd handed over a ten-dollar bill. The top of his nose was wrinkled in a deep frown.

"Just dandy!" she muttered testily under her breath.

"Don't bite *my* head off, you're the one who wanted to play Dick Tracy."

"Yes, but I had no idea I was going to have to take off my clothes."

He looked amused for the first time. "What are you worried about? Is your body particularly gruesome?"

She could hear the laughter in his voice. "That's not funny."

If he hadn't been so worried about her, he would have thought it hilarious. He couldn't have planned it any better. If he got her out of this, she would probably hand over her resignation sooner than he'd hoped.

Ashley bit back a retort as the women returned, each carrying a case of beer. In a matter of minutes, they were back on the road again.

The ride to the lake took about twenty minutes, but seemed an eternity to Ashley, whose back ached from sitting in such a rigid position on the motorcycle. But she would have cut out her tongue before admitting as much to Jack. If she was uncomfortable before, though, it was nothing compared to the bone-jolting ride she received once they'd pulled off the highway and onto a dusty, pockmarked road. She tightened her grip on him and held on.

The bikers parked in front of a run-down house overlooking a small lake. Tall pine trees surrounded the area, making it all very private and secluded. Jack paid scant notice to the scene; his eyes were trained on the three men who'd come out of the house to greet them. His gaze met Ashley's, and he gave a slight nod, so slight, in fact, that Ashley wondered for a minute if she had imagined it.

Ashley accepted a can of beer from a big-boned woman with long dark hair that looked as though it hadn't been washed in weeks. As she paused in front of Jack, her look told him she was willing to give him more than a can of beer. For some reason this annoyed Ashley, and she glared at him.

"You're supposed to be with me," she reminded him in a heated whisper. "The least you can do is stop ogling the women right under my nose."

"Please," Jack muttered, "give me more credit than that." He glanced back at the men, trying to think of his next move. "We have to stay for a while," he said, then grinned at her look of horror. "I think the guy in the green shirt is our man."

Her heart sank. "Then why do we have to stay?"

"Because I'm not sure. I need to get a better look at him. Also, I want to find out if he actually lives here. It would certainly make things easier for my client."

"What am I supposed to do in the meantime?" she asked in a high-pitched voice. Lord, she hated to complain—she'd wanted to impress him. But the situation was getting out of control.

"I'll think of something." He led her down by the lake, where several people had already begun stripping.

Ashley clung to Jack's hand and tried to avoid looking at the naked people standing at the water's edge. She felt ridiculous for being so shy. After all, she would never see them again. But the mere thought of peeling off her clothes in front of the group terrified her. She was surprised when Jack led her well past the others to where a weeping willow hung over the water.

"Okay, this will give you a little privacy," he said. "Strip down to your bra and panties."

"My bra and panties?" She watched in disbelief as he pulled his shirt over his head. Ashley stared for a moment, eyes bulging, taking in the curly brown hair that covered his chest so nicely. Holy mackerel, it was one of the best-looking chests she'd ever seen!

"Well, don't just stand there," he said, kicking off his shoes.

"What are you doing?" she asked breathlessly.

"I'm taking my clothes off. What does it look like I'm doing?"

"You don't have to snap at me," she answered, unbuttoning her blouse with trembling fingers. Gritting her teeth, she pulled the blouse off and tossed it to the ground. Jack's own fingers worked at the fastening of his jeans.

"Are you going to wear your underwear in the water too?" she asked.

"I don't wear underwear."

"Oh." A second later, he proved it.

Ashley snapped her head up and found herself looking into a pair of amused eyes. "I'm glad you find this so funny!" she said, reaching down to unzip her own pants. She shoved them down, her gaze never wavering from his face. She'd be fine, she told herself, as long as she didn't look below his waist.

Jack felt as though his blood was on fire as Ashley's jeans clumped around her trim ankles. There was something to be said for partially clad women, he thought. It left certain pertinent details to the man's imagination, and at that moment his thoughts were running amuck. When he glanced around, he was relieved to see that the bikers seemed intent on their own women. His voice was deceivingly cool when he spoke, and did not vent his concern.

"Hey, it's not Sunday," he said, suddenly pointing at the panties she wore.

Ashley blinked. The man made absolutely no sense. Wasn't it bad enough she had to stand there and look casual while he paraded around in the raw? "What, pray tell, are you talking about?"

"You've got on your Sunday panties, and today is Monday."

Ashley blushed profusely as she looked down at her bikini underwear and saw that the embroidered stitching did indeed read "Sunday." "Well, so what? My Monday panties are in the wash, okay?" He merely shrugged in response, and walked into the water as though it were commonplace for the two of them to be traipsing about in the buff and near-buff. But he was careful to remain in the shadows of the willow.

Ashley tentatively stuck a toe into the water. It was warm. Her gaze fluttered over to where Jack stood with his back to her. She felt her own quick intake of breath as her eyes took in the wide back and narrow hips. He had the broadest shoulders she'd ever seen. His waist was trim, his hips lean and taut, several shades lighter than his toasty sun-kissed body. He was nothing less than magnificent.

"Are you coming in?" He turned around and caught her staring. The smile he gave her was brazen as hell. He held out his hand.

Ashley, her heart jackhammering in her chest, captured it and allowed him to pull her into the tepid water. Thankfully, the weeping willow partially blocked them from view of the others. Jack's thoughtfulness warmed her. "This was a good idea," she said, indicating the tree. "Thank you."

He pulled her closer, and didn't miss the surprised look on her face. "You're supposed to be my woman," he reminded her, as he reached behind her head and pulled a fabric-coated rubber band from her long hair. Using his fingers as a comb, he raked them through her thick hair and pulled it on either side of her shoulders. It fell over the wispy material of her bra. He hoped the fact that he'd kept her partially clad would lead the others to think he was the possessive type.

Ashley was mesmerized by the look on his face. She splayed her hands over his chest and dug her fingers into the springy curls that adorned it. They were just acting, she reminded herself, no longer able to avoid the temptation to touch him. Even so, it was definitely one of the sexiest chests she'd ever seen. And the way the hair whorled around his navel and— No, she shouldn't be thinking along those lines.

Jack leaned forward and kissed the tip of her nose. His chest grazed the front of her bra and caused her nipples to contract. He traced the line of her jaw and stroked one cheek before dropping a kiss on her mouth. When he raised up, he was smiling. "You're the best-looking private-eye's assistant I've ever had," he said.

"We're not getting much work done," she reminded him.

"No, we're not." Without warning, he lowered his head and captured her lips with his. He felt her stiffen in surprise, then slowly relax under the gentle pressure of his mouth. His tongue traced her bottom lip before dipping inside her mouth in search of other goodies. After their tongues had played a leisurely game of cat and mouse, he beckoned her own tongue into his mouth. His hands slid around to her hips and cupped them in his palms, and the feel of nylon covering each firm buttock was almost his undoing.

"Hey, lovebirds, we're leaving," one of the bikers called from the water's edge.

Jack jumped in response and immediately blocked Ashley from view. Lord, what was he doing? He was supposed to be protecting her from the others, and here he was literally ravishing her in front of God and everybody!

"How come you're still wearing your clothes?" asked the biker, obviously having seen that Ashley remained in her underwear. "I ain't seen a biker's woman yet who was scared to take off her clothes."

"She's not shy," Jack said. "I'm jealous. I can't

stand to have another man look at her. Know what I mean?" His tone was deadly and defied argument.

The biker nodded. "I shot a man once for looking at my woman," he said. He made his way back to the group.

Jack felt his body sag with relief as he led Ashley to land and grabbed his clothes, stepping into them quickly. The others were heading toward their bikes. "Go behind those pine trees and get dressed," he said. "I want to have one last look at our host."

Ashley nodded and hurried away. She needed a few minutes to gather her wits. Her head was still spinning from Jack's kiss, and her hands trembled so badly, it was difficult to button her blouse. She was being ridiculous, she told herself. Jack had not meant the kiss in any romantic sense. It was part of the job, the same job that had prompted them to strip in the first place. If she hoped to work for her uncle's agency in the future, she was going to have to get used to surprises.

"It's him," Jack said a few minutes later, as he climbed onto his motorcycle. He could barely contain his excitement at finding the man, or relief that Ashley had come through it unharmed.

"Are you sure?"

"Damn right I'm sure. Get on." All he wanted to do was get the hell out of there.

Ashley climbed onto the motorcycle and snaked her arms around his waist. "What are you going to do?"

"I'm going to notify my client right away, of course." He paused and looked down. "What's that you're holding? It's dripping water all over the front of my pants."

She blushed profusely. "It's my underwear. They were wet, so I took them off."

"Do you mean to tell me you're not wearing *anything* under your clothes?" he asked, feeling his pulse quicken at the thought. His gut tightened. What if someone had seen her?

"That's right."

Jack shook his head, his mouth set in a grim line. It was bad enough he'd worried himself into a frenzy that one of the men would make a pass at her. And it hadn't been easy pretending indifference to her scantily clad body. Now, he had to endure the mental picture of her nude beneath her clothes . . . her bare breasts straining against the cotton blouse she wore. . . . Oh, hell, he wasn't going to be able to concentrate on his driving. Why did the woman insist on doing things that drove him right out of his mind?

Jack kicked the motorcycle to life. He followed the other bikers back onto the highway, all the while cursing himself for bringing Ashley with him to begin with. His plan on scaring her off had failed. He had been the scared one. Now that she had more or less passed the test, she would be even more determined to stay.

When he let her off at her front door some time later, he tried to avoid eye contact. Her underwear was still wadded up in one hand.

"I'm sorry for giving you a hard time over the skinny-dipping part," she said, guessing she probably acted like a first-rate ninny.

"You did fine." He needed a drink. Several, in fact.

"Well—" She paused. "I guess I'll see you tomorrow then."

Tomorrow? He felt his gut tighten at the thought of seeing her again. He was going to have to call Jeeter and tell him he just couldn't go through with it. He couldn't keep his mind on his work when she was around, and he worried about her all the time. "I've got to go," he said a bit roughly. He revved his engine. "See you."

Ashley stared after Jack as he drove down the street and disappeared around the corner. When she entered the house, she found Chip and Mikie in front of the television, where she'd left them.

"What do you have in your hand?" Chip asked the moment he saw her. "It's dripping on the floor."

Ashley chuckled. "You wouldn't believe it if I told you." She made her way toward the laundry room, where she tossed her wet belongings into the washer and plucked a terry-cloth robe from the dryer. What would her son think if he knew his mother had gone skinny-dipping with a group of bikers? And what would he think if he knew she'd actually had a good time—thanks to Jack Sloan. The man sure could kiss. . . .

Three

The following morning, Ashley pulled up in front of her uncle's agency at quarter to seven. The lights were on—obviously Jack was already there. She climbed out of her car and walked toward the building carrying a large grocery sack. When she entered the office, she found Jack sitting at his desk. His hair was still damp, no doubt from his shower, and the gold earring he wore caught the morning light streaming in through the window and winked at her.

"Well, I see you made it on time," he said, noting the freshly ironed khakis she wore. Her crisp ecru blouse, edged with eyelet lace at the neck and sleeves, was pleasantly feminine. Not that she needed anything to boost her femininity, he told himself, remembering how she'd looked the day before in those flimsy garments she called underwear.

"Yes, sir, and I'm raring to go."

"Don't get too excited, Sherlock, we got a while. What's in the paper bag?"

Ashley smiled and reached inside the sack. "All kinds of goodies." She began pulling items out. "I have a Thermos of hot coffee, a box of doughnuts, two tuna-fish sandwiches, a pair of binoculars, and several bars of candy. I brought the binoculars in case you didn't have an extra pair. I would have brought magazines, but I couldn't fit them in the bag."

"Look, lady," he said, "this isn't a field trip. And you won't have time to read magazines. You're going to need your eyes for surveillance work."

Ashley nodded. So she'd made a mistake. Big deal. The man didn't have to go into such a snit about it. She was only trying to make a good impression. "What is our assignment today?" she asked, excited about the prospect of investigative work. If she had managed to get through the events of the previous day, this day would be a cinch.

"We usually have several jobs in one day. I try to arrange them in time slots when we're most likely to see the most action."

"Action?" she asked excitedly.

"When I say action, I don't mean action like they have on TV," he said wryly. "I've never been beat up, and I seldom carry a gun. And when I have carried a gun, I've never had to use it. Still excited?"

"You really do know how to burst a person's bubble, don't you?"

If only she knew, he thought. He'd tried to have her fired the night before, but Jeeter wouldn't hear of it. "Give her a chance, Jack," he'd said. "Do it for me." Jack had been tempted to tell Jeeter about how she'd accompanied him on the case with the bikers and how he'd worried about her. But Jeeter would tell him it was his own fault for taking her along in the first place.

"Before we go to work, I have some books I want you to read," Jack told her. He reached for the stack of books on his desk. He had hunted all over his place that morning to find them. He'd never had time to read them personally. "These books are extremely important in our field of work," he continued in a serious, businesslike voice. "You must know them inside out." He handed her a thick one. "This book explains many of our procedures." He handed her another. "And this one shows pictures of the various equipment we use. As you can see, it's quite extensive." He finally settled the whole lot in her arms.

"I'll get on them right away," Ashley dutifully promised.

"You can start reading this morning," he told her. "I have some personal business to attend to. I'll be back around ten o'clock. That'll give you about three hours of reading." It was difficult to keep from feeling guilty with Ashley looking so eager to please, but if Jeeter wasn't going to change his mind about hiring her, then it was up to him. Perhaps she'd reconsider taking the job if he assigned her enough dull reading.

Jack was grinning when he let himself out the front door a few minutes later. He did feel a little guilty after piling all those books on her, he admitted to himself. Although she hadn't batted an eye at the stack, he'd be willing to bet she was inside at that very moment trying to think of a polite way to quit.

Jack climbed into his car and slammed the door. Yes, he was feeling very pleased with himself at the moment. The pretty lady could play private detective all she wanted, but he was going back to bed. Besides, it was her own fault. He'd lain awake all night thinking about her.

Ashley was well into her books when Jack returned several hours later.

"How's the reading going?" he asked, noting with irritation that she was sitting behind his desk. First day on the job, and she was already taking over. But wasn't that just like a woman? he told himself. Next she'd want to redecorate the office and buy plants. If that wasn't bad enough, Jeeter was moping around as though someone had snatched his chewing tobacco. No doubt he felt sorry for his niece because of all the reading Jack had given her.

"It's going fairly well," Ashley answered, giving him an easy smile. "Good thing I attended all those speed-reading courses."

Jack blinked. "You've taken speed-reading courses?" Jeeter looked surprised, then pleased.

She nodded. "Oh, yes, I've taken quite a number of courses for free while working at the library." She motioned to the stack of books. "This is nothing compared to the reading I did as a librarian."

Jack stood there for several seconds, feeling as though somebody had just punched him in the stomach. He didn't have to look at Jeeter to know the man was grinning from ear to ear. It was obvious

Jeeter would lie down and die for his niece. "We'd better get to work," Jack said. "My car is outside."

"Where's your bike?"

"I left it at home."

Jeeter looked up from the morning newspaper he was reading. "Oh, Jack, I heard about the case you two worked on yesterday." He chuckled. "Ashley told me all about it."

"Even the skinny-dipping part," she added laughingly. "It wasn't funny at the time, but it's hilarious now."

"Yeah, it was a real blast," Jack muttered. "Can we go now?"

"Sure, Jack," she said brightly, grabbing her purse as she stood. Ashley waved to her uncle. "I'll see you at dinner tonight." She followed Jack out the door.

Ashley was markedly excited when she climbed into Jack's car with her grocery bag a few minutes later. "What kind of job are we going on?" she asked.

"First thing we have to do is follow a woman. Her husband, my client, claims she's running around on him. He's probably right."

"What makes you say that?"

"Because you can't trust women."

"Boy, somebody really broke your heart, didn't she?"

"My heart has nothing to do with it," he said, reaching for his seat belt. He fastened it. "It's a well-known fact that men and women just can't stay faithful to one another. Believe me, I've been in this business long enough to know."

Ashley fastened her own seat belt as Jack started the car and put it into reverse. She wasn't about to argue with him. He sounded awfully bitter.

Jack pulled out onto the main road and glanced at Ashley, wondering why she'd become so quiet. Perhaps he shouldn't have barked at her. She was certainly entitled to her opinion. He had to admit she was bright, not to mention good-looking. She'd plaited her hair into a thick braid, which hung down her back and made her look younger than she was. He remembered how silky that same hair had felt the day before when he'd touched it, and now he itched to feel it between his fingers again. As much as he tried, he could not look at her without his gaze dropping to her gently rounded breasts. Those same breasts had strained against the gauzy fabric of her bra the day before. Aw, damn. He shouldn't be thinking along those lines, he told himself. He wouldn't get a blasted thing accomplished.

"I've got a lot of equipment in back," he finally said when she kept looking at him as though she expected him to say something. He wasn't one for idle conversation, but it was better than being left alone with his thoughts, which at the moment centered around the woman next to him. "Always make sure your door is locked before leaving the car."

Ashley nodded. "Could you tell me a little more about this case?"

Jack glanced over at her. She looked excited about the case. He wished she didn't have to get so keyed up. When she did, her eyes sparkled and turned the clearest shade of blue he'd ever seen. And every time she smiled, that begging-to-be-kissed dimple would appear. She had a funny way about her. Every time she looked at something, it was as though she were seeing it for the first time. How could she have gone through a divorce without growing bitter? he wondered.

"My client is certain his wife is running around on him, but he can't catch her. I've been tailing her off and on for several days. The only time she goes out of the house is to buy groceries or go to her health club. And I know she's not messing around with anyone at the health club—it's for ladies only."

"Hmmm."

He looked at her. "What's that supposed to mean?"

"I'm thinking." ·

They rode in a comfortable silence for about twenty minutes before Jack turned onto a quiet-looking street in an upper-class neighborhood. "That's her BMW," he said, passing a brick ranch-style house.

"Where are we going to park?"

"We're not. I already know what time she leaves for the health club, so we'll just meet her there. I just wanted to see which car she was driving today."

Fifteen minutes later, Jack pulled into the parking lot of a prestigious health club and parked on the last row. "Another thing, if you're tailing someone over and over, you've got to be careful about driving the same car all the time. Last time I followed this lady, I drove Jeeter's car. We also have a couple of junkers behind the office that I drive from time to time. Once I had to drive an ice-cream truck, but that's another story."

A few minutes later, Jack sat up straight and looked out the window. "There she is."

"Huh?" Ashley had been counting the cars in the parking lot.

"See the white BMW?"

"I see it." Ashley reached into her bag for the binoculars and raised them to her eyes.

"What the hell do you think you're doing?" Jack demanded, snatching the binoculars from her. "Do you want the whole world to know we're watching her?"

"How am I supposed to see what she looks like?"

"I *already* know what she looks like, I followed her down the bread aisle at the grocery store the day before yesterday."

The man was impossible. How was she supposed to do her job without seeing the person they were following? "You don't like me, do you?"

The question surprised him. He looked over at her and saw that she was waiting for an answer. "Lady, I hardly know you."

"But you don't like me," she said matter-of-factly, "and you wish my uncle hadn't hired me." There, it was finally out in the open.

"That was Jeeter's decision," he said. "I had nothing to do with it."

"But you wish he hadn't hired me just the same. Is it because I'm a woman?"

"That has nothing to do with it. I just prefer working alone. That way I don't have to worry about anyone but myself. Jeeter didn't see it that way."

At least he was honest, Ashley told herself. She really didn't know how to respond. She would just have to show him she was capable of doing the job and looking after herself. She turned her attention back to the BMW, which was parked on the front row. A woman climbed out of the car, closed the door, and locked it, then made her way inside the club.

"How long does she usually stay?" Ashley asked.

"Couple of hours, sometimes three."

"That's an awful long time to be exercising. You say this place is strictly for women?"

"Yeah."

"Who owns it?"

Jack looked up. Surprise rendered him speechless for a moment before a menacing look crossed his face. "Aw, hell," he muttered, then wrenched his door open.

"Where are you going?" Ashley asked.

"Sometimes I amaze myself at just how stupid I can be," he said. "I never considered the possibility she could be seeing someone on the inside."

"That isn't surprising, since this place is for ladies only," she said. When he climbed out of the car, she stopped him. "You can't go in there." She opened her door and climbed out as well. "Why don't I go in and pretend I want to join? That way I can look around without rousing suspicion."

"You'll screw this up. That woman's husband paid a lot of money—"

"I'm not a complete imbecile," she said stiffly, and slammed the door. She stalked toward the building, turning a deaf ear to his protests.

Jack muttered a curse and got back in the car. "Damn interfering woman!" She would spoil everything. He pulled his package of cigarettes out of his pocket and lighted one. No telling how long he would have to wait. If she fumbled the case, he was going to personally wring her neck.

Jack chain-smoked a half-dozen cigarettes before Ashley returned, looking very pleased with herself.

She climbed in on the passenger's side and closed the door.

"Well?" Jack asked after a moment. "Are you going to tell me what happened, or are we going to play twenty questions?"

"The owner of the health club is her boyfriend," she said smugly. And he didn't think she could do the job. Phooey! "She goes inside and disappears through a door that leads upstairs."

Jack swung his head around and looked at the building. "This place has an upstairs?"

"I was surprised too. You can't tell from the outside that it has a second story. I casually asked the instructor where the stairs leading up went, and she informed me the owner had an apartment on the second floor. Lucky for me the woman liked to gossip. As she tells it, our client's wife goes upstairs to visit her lover first, then comes down and exercises."

"Okay," Jack said, starting the engine. "Can you get inside one more time? You'll need to walk in behind her and watch her go up those stairs and personally document the information."

"They gave me a free pass to come back and try the equipment. Is tomorrow too soon?"

"That's fine." He pulled out of the parking lot and onto the main road.

"How did I do?" Ashley asked after a moment. She wondered if he had any idea how important his opinion was to her.

Jack shrugged. "You did okay," he muttered, still irked that he hadn't discovered the truth himself. He rarely missed a detail. The only excuse he could offer himself was that he'd been overloaded with cases for weeks now, which was why Jeeter had run an ad in the newspaper looking for help in the first place. And the fact that he was so attracted to Jeeter's niece would probably put him further behind in his work. "I should have figured it out myself," he finally said, more disappointed with himself than he was willing to admit. Hadn't he learned a long time ago that one little mistake could cost him everything?

"Are you ready for lunch?" Jack asked some time later. It was almost one o'clock.

Ashley nodded. "Don't forget, I brought tuna-fish sandwiches. She didn't catch the expression on Jack's face as she said it.

"I'll drive to a convenience store and buy soft drinks," he said, knowing it would be rude to turn down the sandwich. Surely, there was worse tasting-food in the world than tuna fish?

"And I'll pick up some snacks while we're there. This undercover work makes a person hungry."

Jack glanced over at her in surprise. "Did you eat all those candy bars you brought?"

She nodded lamely. "Why, did you want one?"

He shook his head and lighted a cigarette. Several minutes later, he pulled in front of a store, and they both got out. "If you keep eating all that candy, you're going to get fat," he said, once they were back in the car.

"I never gain weight."

"Then you're in for a big surprise." He started the engine and pulled out of the parking lot. "I know a place where we can eat," he said, watching in amusement as she checked her supply of chocolate.

Soon afterward, Jack parked in front of a small picnic area and cut the engine. "Oh, this is nice," Ashley told him. She got out and followed him to a picnic table, where she handed him one of the sandwiches. He took it without saying a word.

"You don't like tuna fish, do you?" she asked, once he'd taken a couple of bites. He wore the same expression her five-year-old wore when he was forced to eat vegetables.

"I can think of things I hate worse," he muttered. "Like dead animals on the side of the road."

"Jack!"

"You asked."

Ashley shuddered. "You don't have to eat it, you know. I was just trying to be nice by packing a sandwich for you, but I should have learned by now that nothing I do pleases you."

Jack frowned. Was he really so difficult to get along with? he wondered. But he had to admit, even to himself, that he hadn't gone out of his way to be friendly. Perhaps it was because she made him so tense. He worried about her constantly. Jeeter had put a great deal of pressure on him by admitting he didn't trust anybody else with his niece's welfare. "Why should you want to please me?" Jack finally asked. "Your uncle owns the agency."

"I just thought it would be nice if the two of us got along. After all, we're going to be working together. At least until I'm trained," she added.

Not if he had anything to do with it, Jack thought, popping the rest of his sandwich into his mouth.

"Have you ever been married?"

Jack was surprised by the abrupt change of subject. "Why?"

"Just curious."

"Yeah, I was married for a couple of years."

"What happened?"

"We got divorced, that's what happened."

"I mean what happened to cause the split?"

Jack wasn't comfortable with her line of questioning. It was too personal. Why should it matter one way or the other if he'd ever been married or divorced? "Have you ever thought of going to work for the CIA? You ask enough questions, you know."

"I'm serious."

"So am I."

She sighed. "You don't have to answer. And I'm sorry for being so nosy. I guess I'm just a curious person."

"You're telling me." He wadded up his napkin and sandwich bag and tossed them into a nearby trash can. He wondered what it would be like to have a natural sense of curiosity about the world and those around him. Frankly, he didn't give a flying cuss what the next guy did, as long as it didn't affect him. He hadn't always been like that, though, he reminded himself. He had grown hard over the years.

"Any children?"

Jack gave her a blank look. "What?"

"Did you and your ex-wife have children?"

"I thought we were off of that subject." When her eyes continued to question him, he shook his head. "No children, thank God. Now, are you ready to go, Sherlock Holmes? I have to serve some subpoenas, then get back to the office so I can check my messages."

"I'm ready," Ashley replied, disappointed that they

weren't able to communicate as friends. But then again, she thought, perhaps she was better off knowing as little about Jack Sloan the man as possible. He could be too appealing at times, and she certainly wasn't looking to get involved with him, or with any man, at this point in her life.

Jeeter was waiting for them when they returned. "How'd everything go?"

"We got the scoop on Webster's wife," Jack said, taking a seat behind his desk. "It seems the lady is getting more of a workout than she bargained for." Jack filled him in on the details.

Jeeter shook his head. "Why didn't I think of that?"

"I didn't think of it either," Jack said, "and it was staring me right in the face. Your niece figured it out."

Jeeter smiled and winked at Ashley. "Good work, sugar."

For the next couple of days Ashley rode with Jack from early morning till late afternoon. She settled the Webster case by following Mrs. Webster into her health club and personally watching her climb the stairs to her boyfriend's apartment. When the woman came down more than an hour later with the boyfriend in tow, Ashley was pleased to see that several of the women in the club noticed. She would be able to provide more than enough witnesses if Jack thought it necessary. The following afternoon, Jack, looking very respectable in a coat and tie, testified in court for Mr. Webster. Ashley was questioned by the distinguished-looking judge as well, and although she felt bad about the breakup of the Webster marriage, Ashley realized she couldn't afford to become personally involved.

On Friday Jack and Ashley were parked down the street from a house they were watching when Ashley surprised him by lighting a cigarette.

"What the hell are you doing?" he demanded.

She looked at him, the cigarette dangling from between her lips. She took it out with two fingers. "Didn't I tell you? I started smoking."

He sighed heavily. "I suppose you have a perfectly good reason as to why you waited until now to pick up such a nasty habit?" He folded his arms over his chest and waited for an explanation.

"Because I get restless just sitting here," she said. "I've gained five pounds from eating candy bars. I decided smoking was less fattening, and I'll only do it during working hours, just so I won't eat."

He shook his head and muttered a curse. The world was not a simple place as long as the two of them shared it. "Has it come to your attention that I haven't smoked one cigarette all day?" he asked.

"Yes, now that you mention it. So that's why you're so cranky," she said, as though she'd just discovered one of life's best-hidden secrets. "And you've been eating a lot of candy bars."

"That's because I'm dying for a cigarette," he answered, clipping his words. "I quit smoking last night, but you aren't making it easy."

"You should have told me. I'm not a mind reader, you know."

Jack, his patience worn thin by her indifferent

attitude, reached into the small paper sack he'd brought with him and pulled out a chocolate bar. This ought to get her goat, he told himself. He made a production of unwrapping it, certain Ashley's mouth was watering like crazy. He took a bite and chewed, all the while moaning in delight. When he swallowed, he licked his fingers and smacked his lips loudly.

In response, Ashley blew a smoke ring in his face. Pretty good for a beginner, she told herself.

Jack stopped chewing. "Are you going to sit there and blow cigarette smoke in my face?"

"I will as long as you insist on holding chocolate orgies right under my nose."

He wanted a cigarette so bad he could taste it. His head was splitting, and his mouth was bone-dry, no doubt from nicotine withdrawal. He almost growled the next words. "Then take it!" he said, thrusting it in her face.

"I don't want it!" She snatched the candy bar from his hand and tossed it out the open window.

"Why did you do that?" he demanded.

"You deserved it. Not only are you rude, you have the manners of a . . . a slug."

His face went blank. "What the hell is that?"

She glared at him. "It's a mollusk."

"Oh, for Pete's sake!" he bellowed, rolling his eyes heavenward. "This is the most ridiculous conversation I've ever had. Could we please put a stop to this yelling and get on with our work? I have to meet a client."

Ashley sighed. They *were* being ridiculous, she agreed silently. But worse than that, she was being unfair. She had heard how difficult it was to give up smoking, and she knew the poor man was probably having a tough time of it. It certainly explained his dark mood. She was going to have to be patient with him, at least for a few days. If by then his mood wasn't better, she'd clobber him. "Who's the client?" she asked at last.

"You don't know her. She hired me to follow her husband in the evenings. He has been seeing his secretary."

"That's a shame."

They discussed the case as he drove across town, almost as if they had never argued in the first place. Jack pulled into the parking lot of a small restaurant and parked. "I think it would be less embarrassing for my client if I went alone."

Ashley nodded. "I understand." She remained in the car while Jack went inside the restaurant. She watched him through the large plate-glass windows as he walked to a table where a middle-aged woman sat. The look on his face was grim, resigned. He doesn't like this part of his job, Ashley thought. When they exited ten minutes later, neither looked happy. Jack climbed into the car and started the engine.

"How'd she take it?" Ashley asked.

Jack heaved an enormous sigh. No matter how many times he'd had to tell husbands and wives their mates were cheating on them, it still wasn't easy. He knew from experience how devastating it could be. First there was shock, then denial. Once the truth sank in, the pain began. It was the ultimate rejection.

"She's upset, naturally," he told her. "After thirty years of marriage . . ." He left the sentence hanging as he backed out of the parking space.

Ashley watched him for a few minutes. "There's something else. What is it?"

"She wants proof."

"But you gave her proof."

He shook his head. "You don't understand. She wants pictures."

Ashley realized her mouth was hanging open. She closed it. "Pictures? But how? Can you do that?"

"Of course I can do it," he said simply. "I just have to find the right time and place."

Four

Ashley arrived at the office the following morning at
eight o'clock sharp, only to find the front door locked
and Jack nowhere in sight. She had waited twenty
minutes in her car before he drove up.

"I want my own office key," she said as soon as
he'd unlocked the door and let her in.

He avoided looking at her. He didn't want to be
reminded how good she looked in the morning—
fresh, like a rosebud in spring. He paused at his
own train of thought. Rosebud in spring? Where in
the hell had that come from? Lord, if he wasn't
careful, he would be composing sonnets to her before long.

"Talk to Jeeter," he said.

It wasn't until after Ashley had made coffee and
poured herself a cup that she approached him again.
"When am I going to start riding alone?"

Jack looked surprised. "What d'you mean, when
do you start riding alone? You haven't even been

here a week." He shook his head. "Talk to Jeeter. He makes all the decisions around here."

"Talk to Jeeter," she mimicked, and glared when he chuckled under his breath. "How am I supposed to learn anything if the two of you refuse to give me any responsibility?" she demanded. "I don't like being coddled, Jack Sloan." She planted her hands on her hips as Jack stood and made his way purposefully around his desk. Jack placed his hands on her shoulders in an attempt to calm her down.

"Look, we're not going to get anything accomplished by arguing. When your uncle comes in, sit down and give him your complaints. I'm sure he can come up with a solution." Jack tried to ignore the scent of her perfume. He already knew how good she smelled from riding next to her in his car. Her lips were parted in surprise, and he ached to trace them with his finger. Better yet, he wanted to taste them again.

Without warning, Jack pulled her into his arms and captured her lips with his. Ashley felt a wave of shock rush over her, and she was rendered motionless for a moment. When her head finally cleared, she grasped the front of his shirt to steady herself, as Jack's lips performed magic on her own. They were warm and coaxing, prodding her mouth open to receive his tongue. While his hand remained at the back of her neck as though anchoring her in place, a finely muscled arm snaked around her waist and pulled her close.

When Jack broke the kiss a moment later, Ashley's head was reeling. She felt as though her brain had turned to mush. Just as she was about to speak, Jack turned his back to her.

"I'm sorry," he said, taking a deep, shaky breath. "That was dumb."

Ashley didn't know how to respond. Her lips felt damp and swollen; they literally tingled from his kiss. And what a kiss it had been! "What was so dumb about it?" she asked breathlessly.

Jack was prevented from answering when Jeeter walked through the door. He was thankful the man hadn't walked in a moment sooner.

Jeeter grinned when he saw them. "Are you two tearing off each other's heads this morning?" he asked.

"Something like that," Jack said in a barely controlled voice. "We need to talk, Jeeter."

The older man looked up in surprise. "Uh-oh, what happened?" He cut his gaze to his niece.

"I was on my way to the ladies' room anyway," Ashley said, realizing Jack wanted privacy. She disappeared through the door, watching him over her shoulder.

Jeeter looked at Jack. "Well? What is it?"

"It's not working out, Jeeter."

"I thought the two of you were finally getting along."

"That has nothing to do with it. She's in the way. She distracts me from my work."

Jeeter grinned. "She does, does she?"

Jack raked his fingers through his hair. "Stop kidding around, would you? I'm serious."

"Give it time, Jack. Give it time."

Jack knew he was wasting his breath. Although he usually knew how to get what he wanted from Jeeter, this time the older man refused to budge. Jack felt absolutely powerless.

"I'm going to ask her to work all night tonight on

the Jones custody case," Jack said after a minute. "We only have a couple of days before the court date. Who knows? Maybe she'll hate it and quit."

Jeeter didn't look convinced. "Don't count on it, boy."

Both men stopped talking when Ashley walked through the door. "Is it safe to come in?" she asked, her gaze going directly to Jack. No doubt he'd been raking her over the coals in her absence. He was certainly a man of contradictions, she thought. One minute he was kissing her senseless, and the next he was trying to get her booted out. "You feel like working tonight?" Jack asked.

She looked up in surprise. "Do we have a job?"

He nodded. Jeeter pulled himself up from his chair and made his way around the desk. He put his arm around Ashley. "I'm going to leave the two of you alone to discuss the case," he said, "if you'll promise not to hurt each other." He tweaked his niece's nose. "I've got to see a man about a retirement villa."

Ashley was surprised. "Who's retiring?"

"I am."

Her mouth dropped open. "You're not serious?"

Jeeter nodded. "Of course I am. Jack here is going to buy into the business and take over once I'm gone. He pretty much runs the place as it is, especially when my gout is acting up."

Ashley looked from one man to the other. She shouldn't be surprised, she told herself. Her uncle frequently had trouble getting around because of his swollen joints. Still, she hated seeing him give up the career he loved. "I had no idea you were leaving," she finally said.

Jack didn't miss the look of love and concern on

Ashley's face. It was obvious she was crazy about her uncle. He couldn't help but wonder how it would feel to have those emotions channeled toward him. Not that it was likely, he told himself. But it was on his mind much of the day as he and Ashley delivered a backlog of subpoenas and gave lie-detector tests to potential employees of a large chemical company.

"What time do you want me to meet you back here tonight?" Ashley asked at the end of the day.

"Why don't you plan on being here around midnight," he told her. "It's a custody case, and we're trying to get some dirt, anything, on the child's mother."

"Oh?"

"Yeah. The only thing we have against her is the fact that her boyfriend spends the night at the house quite often in the presence of the children. We want to get pictures of his car sitting in the driveway all night, but I especially want to get pictures of him leaving the morning after."

"Will that prove her unfit?"

"It won't prove her unfit, but it'll make her look bad in court."

"I don't like the sound of this case."

"You don't have to like it. It's just another job." He wondered for a moment if she might back out.

"I'll be here," she muttered, as she climbed out of the car and slammed the door behind her.

Ashley arrived home and found Mikie had been sick much of the afternoon. Chip had made a bed on the couch so his younger brother could watch cartoons. Ashley checked his temperature and saw that he had a slight fever. She looked in the medicine cabinet for something to bring it down.

Once Ashley had doctored her son, she put a casserole in the oven and straightened the house. When dinner was ready, she convinced Mikie to take a few bites of the meal before she and Chip sat down to eat. "I have to work tonight," she told Chip.

Chip looked surprised and a bit piqued. "Don't you put in enough time as it is?"

"It's only for a few hours," she said, noting how old her son looked with a frown wedged between his dark brows. Both boys had inherited her dark hair and olive complexion. "Stop worrying, Chip," she said, reaching over to pat his hand affectionately.

"I can't help it. Somebody has to worry about you," he said softly.

"I'm a grown woman. I can take care of myself."

It was close to midnight when Ashley parked her car next to Jack's in front of the agency. Light spilled from the windows. She felt rested and alert after the nap she'd taken. At least she wouldn't fall asleep on the job, she hoped. Ashley twisted around in her seat and checked her sleeping son before she got out of the car and pushed the door closed gently.

Jack was on the telephone when Ashley entered the office. Talking to a woman, no doubt, she told herself. He hung up the telephone and glanced at her. "Ready to go?"

"I have my five-year-old with me," Ashley said, squaring off for an argument. Jack had not impressed her as a big fan of children, and she was certain he would frown on her bringing a sick child to work with her.

"Any particular reason?"

"He has a fever. I was afraid to leave him."

"Why didn't you stay home?" Personally, Jack had wanted to stay home. He was dead on his feet. He had planned to catch some Z's before meeting her, but he'd been called in for a late appointment and had decided to stay and catch up on paperwork. He was wired, having drunk a whole pot of coffee, and he desperately wanted a cigarette. His mood was not good.

"I didn't want to give you another reason to complain about me to my uncle."

He gave a snort of a laugh. "Oh, now you're going to make me out to be a bad guy."

"I didn't say that." But she wasn't going to deny it. "If you don't mind, I'd like to move him to the backseat of your car."

Jack shook his head as he followed Ashley out the front door. He would have preferred she stay home and care for her sick child, but there was no sense arguing about it. She could be as stubborn as her uncle when she wanted. He paused a moment to shut off the lights and lock the door, then hurried to her car. "I'll pick him up," he said, once he'd looked in on the sleeping boy. "You run over and unlock my car." He handed her his keys.

Once they had Mikie installed in the backseat with his blanket and pillow, Jack and Ashley climbed in front. She waited until they were out of the parking lot before she spoke.

"Do you work many nights?" she asked, her voice low so as not to wake Mikie.

He shrugged. "Here and there."

Not much of an answer, she thought. "So, you're going to take over the business when Jeeter retires."

The abrupt change in subject caught him by surprise. He glanced at her. "Looks that way."

"I'll bet you've always wanted to have your own agency," she said. In the beginning he hadn't impressed her as being the ambitious type. Once she began riding with him, though, she discovered what a' hard worker he was. "Haven't you?" she added when he didn't answer.

He stifled a yawn. It was going to be a long night. All he could think about at the moment was climbing into his nice, comfortable bed. "Yeah, I guess," he finally mumbled.

"What stopped you?"

Damn but she asked a lot of questions. It was times like these that he wished he still smoked. "Lack of money, what else?"

"Are you going to turn it into a big agency, or keep it the size it is?"

He clasped his head with his hands. "Are you going to keep asking me questions, or wait till I commit suicide by jumping out my window headfirst?"

"Sorry!" Ashley snapped her head around and stared out her window. "I was just trying to carry on a conversation. You have to be one of the most secretive persons I've ever met," she said.

"Lady, you ask more questions than the feds. And could you lower your voice, so you don't wake up the kid? The last thing I want on my hands right now is a sick kid."

Ashley folded her arms across her breasts. "Sometimes I can't imagine why my uncle hired you."

"Because I'm good, that's why."

Ashley didn't have to look at him to know he was grinning. She wondered if he had purposely dropped the double entendre in her lap, or if it had been accidental. Her thoughts ran amuck with possibilities that had absolutely nothing to do with detective work. She felt her cheeks flame in the darkness. She was vaguely aware when Jack turned into a middle-class neighborhood and parked in front of a small brick house.

"Is this the place?" When he nodded, she looked at him in surprise. "You're going to park right out front?"

"Yep."

She waited for an explanation, but he didn't offer one. "Would you mind telling me why? I mean, we usually aren't so . . . conspicuous."

Jack shrugged. "I've already got what I want. See that Oldsmobile? It belongs to the woman's boyfriend. Since it's after midnight and the house is dark, it's safe to assume he's sleeping there. I just want to be here when he decides to go home. How's the kid doing back there?"

Ashley reached around and touched her son's forehead. "Feels like his fever is down. He's not due medicine for several more hours."

"My mother used to put onions on the soles of my feet to bring a fever down."

"Did it work?"

"Beats me. All I know is it stank to high heaven." Jack slid down in the seat and positioned his back against the door. "Might as well get comfortable," he told her. "We're going to be here for a while. This is where private detective work gets boring."

Ashley rearranged herself in the front seat, thankful her son was sleeping soundly. "What's the most exciting or scariest job you've ever been on?" she asked, hoping to draw him into conversation. It would certainly help pass the time. She could barely make out his profile in the dark.

"The time I tried to serve a subpoena on a guy and he stuck a gun in my face had to be the spookiest experience," he said. "Thank goodness he decided not to use it."

"You were lucky."

"That kind of thing doesn't happen very often. You'd be surprised how routine this work can be. Like now." He closed his eyes.

"Did you ever have anything funny happen?"

When Jack spoke, she could tell he was smiling. "It happened when I was just a rookie in this business. I was looking for somebody, and I parked down the street from the house where this person was supposed to be staying. When nobody came out after a couple of hours, I decided to have a look. I climbed a six-foot fence so I could get a view from the back. Lo and behold, I was attacked by two Chihuahuas."

Ashley laughed. "You mean those tiny dogs that resemble rats?"

"It doesn't matter how big they were," he said. "Dropping over that fence was like diving into the Amazon River, piranha and all."

"What did you do?"

"I scaled the fence in about three seconds, when it had taken five minutes to climb over it. You know, those dogs have real high-pitched barks. I swear you can hear them in the next county." He chuckled as he remembered the incident. For some reason her questions weren't bothering him, despite his tiredness. It surprised him that she was so interested in his life.

"What made you choose this line of work?"

"What made you decide to become a librarian?" he asked. "Not that you look like any librarian I ever saw, what with those braids in your hair. You look like you're right out of high school." He paused. "I like your hair." He stated it simply and honestly.

Ashley was surprised by the compliment, but then again, she really wasn't. She had caught him watching her from time to time. Occasionally, when their gazes met, she felt as though a raw electrical wire were pulsing through her body. It was a ridiculous thought for a thirty-five-year-old woman to have, she told herself.

"Thank you," she finally said.

"You're welcome."

A companionable silence fell over them. "Have you ever watched a sunrise?" she asked after a while.

"Many times." He wasn't going to confess he'd watched many of them from the backseat of his car with a woman beside him. 'Course, that had been in his younger days.

"I can remember way back to my senior prom, when a bunch of us spread blankets on a hilltop and watched the sun come up. I remember telling myself it wasn't just a new day I was looking forward to, but a new life as well."

"Hmm. That's deep."

She laughed. "It *was* deep for a high school student. I had a good part-time job. I was signed up for fall classes at our community college. I owned my own car. Those are big-time responsibilities for an eighteen-year-old."

"I don't ever remember being eighteen."

"How could you forget something like that? It's a special time in your life."

"It wasn't for me. I was supporting my mother and my brothers and sisters long before that age. It wasn't likely that I would go to college, since we couldn't even pay the electric bill."

Ashley felt her face grow warm. "I'm sorry, Jack. I suppose not everybody had the idyllic childhood I had."

Now why had he gone and told her all that? he wondered. She'd probably start feeling sorry for him, and the last thing he wanted from her was sympathy. Or maybe she'd figure out the truth, how he'd secretly resented having to give up his dreams in order to support his family. "That's okay," he said, trying to sound indifferent. "It was probably good for me."

Ashley leaned back in the seat and closed her eyes. When she opened them again some time later, the sky had grown lighter. She must've drifted off to sleep. She could make out Jack's silhouette in the gray light. He was holding an odd-looking gadget that resembled binoculars in his hand.

She yawned wide. "What are you doing?"

"Taking pictures."

"In the dark?"

"Yeah, in the dark. I'm glad you grabbed a nap, you looked tired. Feel better?"

She nodded, but she was more interested in what he was doing. "What *is* that thing?"

"It's an infrared viewing system. It takes pictures at night. I want to get a shot of the boyfriend's car and license-tag number."

Ashley reminded herself that it was just a job. The fact that she didn't approve of what they were doing didn't matter in the least. She twisted around in her seat to check on Mikie, who was still asleep. She touched his forehead and found it cool.

"How is he?" Jack asked, reaching for the Thermos she'd brought.

"Cool as a cucumber."

"Good. Want some coffee? We still have a while before the sun comes up."

She nodded and reached inside her paper sack for two Styrofoam cups. When Jack poured her a cup, she thanked him and took a sip. "Do you think he'll be mad when he finds us taking pictures of him as he comes out the front door?"

Jack chuckled. "Wouldn't you be?"

"He won't try to hurt us, will he?"

Jack shook his head. "We'll be out of here so fast, he won't know what hit him. Why do you think I parked the car facing the main road? I plan to snap a picture, then clear out."

They sipped their coffee, lost in their own thoughts, as the sun slowly lifted in the sky, painting it a soft mauve. To Ashley, the hours seemed to crawl by.

"Look at that," Jack said, pointing toward the house. "Somebody just moved the curtain to look out the window. They know we're here."

Ashley glanced in that direction. "Are you sure?"

"I'm sure," he said, pulling his camera from between his feet on the floor. He perked up suddenly. "Wait a minute."

"What is it?"

Jack aimed his camera at the front door as it

opened. "Come to Papa," he said, as a man wearing a three-piece suit walked out, shielding his face from the camera as he made his way to one of the cars in the driveway. "You can try to hide, mister," Jack shouted, "but I still got a picture of your ugly face."

All of a sudden, the man turned around and glared at the two of them. In a split second Jack got the full-face picture he needed, but then the man threw down his briefcase and stalked toward the car, a murderous look on his face.

"What's he doing?" Ashley cried, reaching over to lock her door.

"He's coming after us, what d'you think he's doing?" Jack tossed her the camera, reached for the key in the ignition, and turned it. The car came to life. But the man pursuing them was faster. He took a running leap toward the car and fell on the hood with a loud thud. Ashley screamed as he pounded his fists against the windshield.

"Damn idiot!" Jack roared, and leaned against the horn. "Get off of my car! Look at that, he's bending my damn windshield wipers. I don't believe this guy."

Jack continued to blow his horn. In the backseat Mikie came wide awake and sat up. "Why is that man pounding on the car, Mommy?" he asked.

Ashley's head snapped up. "Honey, crouch down on the floor behind my seat," she said frantically. "Mr. Sloan will take care of everything." She watched in disbelief as the red-faced man attacked the car's antenna, bending it until it snapped off at the base.

"Who does he think he is, destroying my car?" Jack demanded, reaching for the door handle. "I'm gonna take him apart—"

Ashley grabbed Jack by the arm, sinking her fingernails into his flesh. "Don't you *dare* open that door!"

Jack jumped in surprise. "But he's tearing up my car!"

"I have a five-year-old son in the backseat!" she reminded him in a shrill voice. "Get us out of here!"

Jack snapped to attention. He'd forgotten about the kid. "I'm not going to let anything happen to you and the kid, okay? Just hang on, I'll try to get rid of him." Jack hit the gas, and the man fell against the windshield. Then, without warning, Jack stepped on the brake. The man slid right off the car and rolled several times on the ground before he came to a stop. Jack stepped on the accelerator, swerved around the man, and took off down the road, the tires squealing as amazed neighbors looked on.

Ashley didn't give a sigh of relief until they were completely out of the neighborhood and back on the main road. She twisted around in her seat and helped Mikie from the floor. "Are you okay?" she asked breathlessly.

The boy nodded. "Who was that man?" he asked.

Jack tossed him a smile over his shoulder. "Oh, that was a friend of mine. He wanted a lift into town, but I didn't have time to take him. Some people just can't take no for an answer, know what I mean?"

Jack pulled into the parking lot of the agency twenty minutes later and parked next to Ashley's car. "Don't worry about coming in today," he said. "Try to get some sleep."

Ashley yawned. "What are you going to do?"

"First I'm going to an auto-parts store and see if I can replace the parts that guy tore off my car."

Ashley couldn't help but smile. "And you said this job was dull."

Jack regarded his twisted windshield wipers. "Maybe I spoke too soon."

"Mommy, I'm hungry."

"That's a good sign," she said. "You must be feeling better."

Jack and Ashley opened their doors simultaneously and got out of the car. Ashley helped her son out of the backseat and closed the door. When she looked up, her gaze locked with Jack's.

"How 'bout I buy you and the kid breakfast?" Jack suggested, stuffing both hands into his pockets. "It's the least I can do after Freddy Kruger attacked my car with you two in it." It sounded plausible, he thought. He wanted the invitation to sound as if he were trying to make up for what had happened earlier. The last thing he wanted her to think was that he was asking for a date. But the fact was, he wasn't ready to say good-bye to her just yet. Silly as it sounded, he'd felt strangely protective toward her and her son when that lunatic had attacked his car. The thought that either had been in danger had jolted him to the soles of his feet. That kind of thinking was not in his best interest, he told himself. That was just the kind of thinking women liked to hear, the ol' dragon-slayer and damsel-and-child-in-distress routine. A man could find himself in trouble before he knew it.

"You don't have to do that," Ashley said.

"I know I don't *have* to. But your kid is starving, and *somebody* has to feed him. Right, kid?"

Mikie nodded. "Yeah, somebody has to."

Ashley told herself she was doing it for Mikie, and that it had absolutely nothing to do with the way Jack was looking at her or the way she was feeling—her knees weak and trembly, her stomach all soft and mushy like the gooey insides of a candy bar.

"You're right," she said, laughter bubbling up from her throat. "Somebody has to feed him."

Five

"Where are we going?" Ashley asked several days later, as Jack drove some distance north of Atlanta. The sun was low in the horizon, and the sky was dark with the threat of rain.

Jack glanced over at her and couldn't help but appreciate the picture she made with her long hair hanging down her shoulders and back. What man wouldn't enjoy running his fingers through that dark mane, he asked himself, or feeling it brush against his naked body? As always, he tried to steer his thoughts in another direction, but not before a hot flush spread over his body and stoked the fire low in his belly that often blazed when Ashley was near.

"Remember the woman who wanted pictures of her husband cheating?" he asked after a few minutes. "We're going to get those pictures now." He hoped she didn't notice the sudden husky timber of his voice, or discover in his face the full gamut of his desire. He fantasized about her often. Not only did it make for long, sleepless nights, it heightened the tension between them, making them more keenly aware of each other in a physical sense. He paused and looked at the sky. "I only hope the rain holds off," he added.

"It looks more like a thunderstorm to me."

Jack turned onto a road leading up a mountain and smiled at the surprised look she shot him. "We might as well take in a little sight-seeing as well," he said, guiding the car easily around the sharp curves. She was dying to know more, and it amused him. She would give him time to explain, then jump in with questions when he didn't. He liked that about her. Try as she might, her spirit and natural sense of curiosity could not be harnessed. She was definitely not the stuff your typical librarian was made of. He understood now why she'd been desperate for a career change.

"For some reason I get the impression you haven't told me everything," she said in an attempt to pry information from him.

Jack grinned. "It just so happens our friend is part-owner of a cabin in the mountains. His wife, our client, was not aware of this."

"How on earth did you find out about it?"

Another grin. "Jeeter isn't the only one with friends in high places. Anyway, I drove out here the other day and found the cabin. Nobody was there. It's hidden deep in the woods. There's only one road leading in or out, but I don't want to be seen using it. We'll have to park some distance away and cut through the woods on foot. I just hope the lovebirds are together."

"We're going to walk through *those* woods?" She

eyed the thicket of growth doubtfully. "I hope you brought a machete. Anyway, what makes you think they'll be together?"

"He told his wife he was going out of town, but his travel agent says he hasn't heard from him."

A few minutes later, Jack pulled off onto a dirt road and parked. "The cabin should be on the other side of that hill," he said, pointing. "Are you coming?"

Ashley didn't miss the challenging look he gave her. "Of course I'm coming." She opened her door and stepped out. She could literally smell the moisture in the air, but it was difficult to see the clouds through the trees. Once Jack grabbed what equipment he would need, he locked the doors to the car, and they started off. They hadn't gone more than a hundred yards before the rain began.

"You're not going to melt," he told Ashley when she gave him a murderous look. "Besides, I told you to expect anything in this job."

Ashley combed her damp hair away from her face with her fingers. "Is that your way of telling me I should have worn a raincoat?"

Jack chuckled as he continued climbing the hill. By the time they reached the top, the rain was coming down harder. The trees had thinned out, no longer providing a buffer against the rain. He didn't have to look at Ashley to know she was soaked to the skin. If this didn't run her off, nothing would. But then, he wasn't in a hurry to get rid of her anymore.

"How much further is this cabin?" she asked breathlessly, then winced when her white running shoes sank into mud.

"We're getting close now."

"That's what you said fifteen minutes ago."

"Patience, patience."

"That's easy for you to say, your pants don't have to go to the dry cleaners."

"You should dress like me," Jack tossed back, obviously amused at the situation.

"I don't own a pair of jeans that ratty," she said.

"Are you trying to tell me I look like a slob?" When she didn't answer, he went on, "Do you prefer men who dress in business suits and shave every day?"

She was prevented from answering when he stopped abruptly and placed a finger against his lips. "The cabin is on the other side of those trees," he said. He hadn't got the words out of his mouth when the sky opened and let loose a torrential downpour. Ashley jumped when lightning flashed and thunder clapped loudly in its wake and echoed off the mountaintop. Jack grabbed her hand and dragged her in the direction of the cabin.

By the time they reached the clearing where the cabin sat, the sky was spitting pea-size hail onto them. Jack led Ashley to an outbuilding in back of the cabin. Thankfully, the door was unlocked. He shoved her inside.

For a moment the only sound was their ragged breathing. "Are you okay?" Jack finally asked.

Ashley nodded. She could barely see him in the darkness. "Yes, I'm fine. But I may as well tell you, I'm terrified of storms. I'm especially afraid of lightning and hail and strong winds."

"Yeah, well, that pretty much covers all the bases. You should have waited in the car."

"No thanks," she muttered. "If I'm going to do this job, then I'll just have to get over some of my . . . uh . . . timidity."

"You still talk like a librarian sometimes, you know that? Not that that's bad. It gives you different textures." Jack opened the door long enough to take a look outside. "The rain is slowing, and it's starting to get dark. We'll be able to slip out soon."

Ashley was still trying to figure out if he'd just complimented her. It had certainly *sounded* like a compliment. It was foolish to hope for more out of their relationship than he was willing to give or capable of giving. Heaven knew he had enough women vying for his attention. It was no surprise. He was so very . . . male. Yet, there was an underlying sensitivity about him, a gentleness that told her he was very much attuned to a woman's needs. That thought made her stomach flutter wildly, as though a small hummingbird had taken up residence there.

She had developed an odd habit of storing all the nice things he said to her each day in the back of her mind. Each night in bed, she replayed them in her thoughts, examining them, even testing them on her tongue. It was silly and very foolish, but she couldn't help herself.

"How are we going to get back to the car in the dark?" she asked after a moment. Surely, they wouldn't retrace their paths through the woods in the blackness of night. The mere thought conjured up images of wet, slithery creatures just waiting . . . No, she wouldn't think of that.

"We'll have to take the road and hope nobody sees us. If we spot headlights coming our way, we'll hide behind a tree. I have a flashlight in my bag."

"Jack, why do you suppose this man is running around on his wife?" she asked. "I mean, I got a look at her the other day, and I thought she was very attractive."

Jack shrugged in the dark. "Boredom," he said matter-of-factly.

"That doesn't sound like a good enough reason to chance ruining a marriage that has lasted thirty years!"

"I don't make the rules in this game, Sherlock. I told you before, men and women just can't stay faithful to one another."

"I was faithful to my ex-husband."

"That's because you didn't know any better."

"I took my marriage vows seriously," she said, indignant.

"Yeah, and look where it got you. You're raking and scraping to take care of your kids all by yourself. Not only that, your house needs painting, and there isn't a soul to help you."

"What does painting my house have to do with it?"

He sighed. "I'm just trying to show you that your faithfulness to your old man doesn't mean squat in the end."

Ashley felt her cheeks burn. "It certainly meant something to me," she said acerbically. "But then I don't expect you'd know much about honor and responsibility, not to mention love."

"I wrote the book on love, darlin'."

"Oh, give me a break! The only emotion you're aware of is outright lust, and come to think of it, I'm not sure lust can be classified as an emotion."

He chuckled. He could clearly make out her profile in the dark. Her perfume, as subtle as it was, made him think about his favorite things—a fire in winter, a Sunday picnic, a gentle summer rain.

"What's so funny?" she asked.

"I was just thinking, a man could never grow bored with you."

Ashley was more than a little surprised. "I can't believe my ears," she said. "Did I just hear Jack Sloan, lord of one-night-stands, condone monogamy?"

"Lady, I haven't the foggiest idea what you just said. I was just trying to tell you you were good-looking." He reached up and touched her cheek lightly with his index finger, then traced the delicate line of her jaw. "Anyway, what makes you think I'd go for one-night-stands? It's too risky, as far as I'm concerned."

Ashley's heart played a thunderous drumroll, announcing to the rest of her body that Jack Sloan had just turned her knees to putty and short-circuited her central nervous system. She stood completely still as he outlined her face with the gentle, featherlike strokes of his fingers. He had stepped closer, much closer, and she could hear his breathing in the dark, feel his warm breath on her cheek.

"Jack?"

"I'm here, darlin'." He reached around and stroked her damp hair with those same fingers, then raised a handful of the dark mane to his nose. "I like the way your hair smells," he said, inhaling the herbal scent of her shampoo. He cupped the back of her head in his palm and pulled her close. When he lowered his lips to hers, Ashley was waiting.

He tasted of mint, Ashley thought, then remembered it was the gum he chewed to kick his smoking habit. His kiss was more of a caress. Lord, but the man knew how to use those lips of his, and her own lips responded eagerly when his tongue beckoned them apart. Once she had opened herself to him, that same bold tongue explored the cushioned depths inside. Ashley raised a hand to his face and touched his cheek, trailing her fingers across the stubble of his beard. There was something to be said about men who seldom shaved.

The kiss deepened, and Jack folded his arms around her, suddenly hungry for the taste and feel of her. She was sweetness through and through, from her full lips to the smooth column of her throat. When Jack released her, he was shocked and surprised to find himself trembling. The kiss had affected him more than he wanted to admit.

Again, the only sound was their breathing, but it was quick and raspy and uneven now. Jack stepped back, wanting to distance himself from her. Holding her was like biting off a piece of heaven. It made him want more. She felt fragile in his arms, despite her tall, slender build. He could only imagine how good she'd feel in his bed, warm and pliant and . . . Damn! She was as habit-forming as those cigarettes he craved.

He should offer her an explanation, Jack told himself, either apologize or try to rationalize his actions —he was always reaching for her, it seemed, pulling her into his arms. Talk about unprofessional! But sometimes he couldn't help himself, any more than he could help taking his next breath. It frightened him, this feeling of helplessness, but he wasn't ready to admit it and make himself vulnerable to another human being. Not just *any* human being, he reminded himself. This was Ashley—beautiful, stubborn, complex Ashley. And he wasn't getting a drop of work done because he couldn't stop thinking about her.

Jack cracked the door open and glanced out of the shed. "It's dark enough now," he whispered.

Ashley couldn't help but wonder how he could sound so normal after the mind-jolting kiss they'd just shared. She was trembling from head to toe, her body crying out for more. No doubt it meant more to her than to him. He probably swapped kisses the way most men exchanged business cards. The thought depressed her.

"What are we going to do?" she asked, hiding her emotions behind a question.

"I want to check the windows and see if I can get some pictures of them together."

"Isn't that illegal? Peeping into windows, I mean."

"I'll have to check on that and get back to you," he said, pushing the door open slowly.

"You were a cop for ten years and you don't know if peeping into people's windows is illegal?"

Jack came to a complete stop and turned to her. "Look, I've been known to bend a few rules now and then for my clients. Now could we possibly discuss this some other time?"

Ashley clamped her mouth shut in irritation. Wasn't it just like a man to try to kiss a woman senseless, then treat her as though her brains had left her body via her ears! "Pardon me for asking!"

Jack slipped out of the cabin and moved stealthily across the clearing with Ashley right on his heels. Once they reached the log cabin, Jack pressed his back against the roughly hewn logs and motioned for Ashley to do the same. After a moment he began checking windows.

"They're on the couch in the living room," Jack whispered so low that Ashley thought she'd imagined it.

"What are they doing?" she said.

Jack rolled his eyes heavenward. "What do you *think* they're doing?" He tossed her a look over his shoulder. "And you're allowed to use your imagination on this one, Sherlock."

She blushed. "Forgive me. My mind doesn't run along the same gutters as yours."

"Actually, it looks as though they've just finished what they were doing. Right now they're sharing a cigarette." Jack unzipped his shoulder bag and brought out a small, funny-shaped camera, and while Ashley stared in disbelief, he moved to the window and snapped several pictures. Once finished, he slipped the camera back in the bag and zipped it. He looked satisfied.

"That's the most disgusting thing I've ever seen," Ashley said, pursing her lips in distaste.

"You're not being fair," he replied. "You've only been on the job for a couple of weeks. It gets much worse than this." He turned for the road. "Ready to go?"

They walked in silence for the next few minutes as they picked their way through the shadows beside the road. "I guess I do sound rather naive to you, don't I, Jack?" Ashley didn't wait for him to answer. "I still believe in fairy-tale marriages where husbands and wives treat their vows as something true and sacred and meaningful." Her throat constricted with emotion. What a fool she must sound to him. "And there's this little girl in me who still wants to be cared for and cherished by a man, no matter what all these more worldly, sophisticated women want. And I want a man who still has some of that little boy left in him and . . . and I know this all sounds utterly ridiculous to you." Her voice trembled, and a lone tear slid down her cheek like a fat raindrop.

They had stopped walking. Jack spied the tear-drop in the moonlight and caught it with the tip of his finger. He hated to see her cry.

Before Jack could contemplate his next move, he pulled her into his arms. "I'm sorry," he said thickly. "I suppose most people don't view the world as I do." He smiled and placed a finger beneath her chin. When he raised her face to his, he was overcome with emotion.

"Don't ever change, Ashley Rogers," he said. "It's people like you who inspire the rest of us hardened souls." He smiled gently and kissed the tip of her nose.

"You're a helluva woman, you know that? And one day you're going to meet a man who'll make a wonderful husband and father." When she didn't respond, he went on, "He'll be a tax adjuster or an insurance salesman, something respectable. He'll wear three-piece suits and take Mikie to the ball game and help Chip with his girl problems. He'll paint your house for you."

"You're awfully worried about my house needing painting, aren't you?" Ashley sniffed loudly. Jack offered her the tail of his T-shirt, and she dabbed her eyes on it.

"I don't want someone around just to paint and baby-sit my children, Jack," she said, sounding suddenly glum. "When you put it that way, it all sounds rather dull, doesn't it?"

Jack threw his head back and laughed. "Living with you would be about as dull as a Fourth of July celebration." He tucked her hand in the crook of his elbow. "C'mon, we'd better get going."

It started to rain again before they reached the car. Jack unlocked Ashley's door, then hurried around and climbed in beside her. "Your hair is dripping wet," he said.

She nodded. "My son is definitely going to ask questions tonight. I arrived home holding my underwear after my first assignment. This time I look like a wet stray dog."

"You can come by my place and dry your hair," he suggested. "And my landlady has a washer and dryer. I could dry your clothes."

"My clothes should dry soon," she said, "but my hair will take forever. I think I'll take you up on your offer to use your blow dryer, if you're sure you don't mind."

They discussed several cases as they rode to Jack's place, which turned out to be a couple rooms in a boardinghouse. Ashley was clearly surprised. "You live *here*?" she asked, her voice ringing with disbelief as she followed him down a dimly lighted hallway.

Jack unlocked a door at the far end of the hall and pushed it open. "What's wrong with it? I know it's not fancy—"

"Fancy has nothing to do with it, Jack. It's just . . . it's not a home."

Jack closed the door and looked around. "I have everything I need. And there's a kitchenette through that door. They also clean my room and give me fresh towels every day."

"But don't you *want* to live in a house like normal people?" she asked, still wondering why anyone would want to live within the confines of two small rooms.

"No, I don't want to live in a house," he answered matter-of-factly. "I don't like to cut grass or work in a garden or take out the trash or any of the other jobs that come with owning a house. I simply do not want the responsibility."

Ashley nodded slowly. "Yes, I see now that you don't."

They stood there for a moment in silence. "I suppose I should go ahead and dry my hair so I can get home," she said.

Jack showed her where the bathroom was and handed her a portable hand dryer. While she dried her hair, he went into the kitchen and put on a pot of coffee. When Ashley's hair was dry, she joined Jack in the main room. She thanked him for the coffee and took a seat on the sofa while he sprawled out on the bed. After she'd been rained on twice in one evening, the coffee was just what she needed. His thoughtfulness warmed her too.

Ashley took in her surroundings. Although the carpet looked new, the drapes and bedspread were faded and outdated. A lone picture hung over the bed. "What was it like being on the police force?" she asked, wanting to know more about the man who had become so much a part of her daily life. She was not prepared for the hard look Jack gave her. "You don't have to tell me if you don't want to," she added quickly.

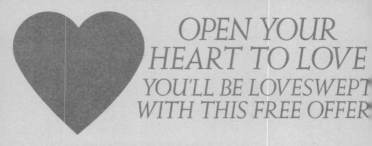

OPEN YOUR HEART TO LOVE
YOU'LL BE LOVESWEPT WITH THIS FREE OFFER

HERE'S WHAT YOU GET:

1. **FREE! SIX NEW LOVESWEPT NOVELS!** You get 6 beautiful stories filled with passion, romance, laughter, and tears...exciting romances to stir the excitement of falling in love... again and again.

2. **FREE! A BEAUTIFUL MAKEUP CASE WITH A MIRROR THAT LIGHTS UP!**
What could be more useful than a makeup case with a mirror that lights up*? Once you open the tortoise-shell finish case, you have a choice of brushes...for your lips, your eyes, and your blushing cheeks.
*(batteries not included)

3. **SAVE! MONEY-SAVING HOME DELIVERY!** Join the Loveswept at-home reader service and we'll send you 6 new novels each month. You always get 15 days to preview them before you decide. Each book is yours for only $2.09 — a savings of 41¢ per book.

4. **BEAT THE CROWDS!** You'll always receive your Loveswept books before they are available in bookstores. You'll be the first to thrill to these exciting new stories.

BE LOVESWEPT TODAY — JUST COMPLETE, DETACH AND MAIL YOUR FREE-OFFER CARD.

FREE – LIGHTED MAKEUP CASE!
FREE – 6 LOVESWEPT NOVELS!

- NO OBLIGATION
- NO PURCHASE NECESSARY

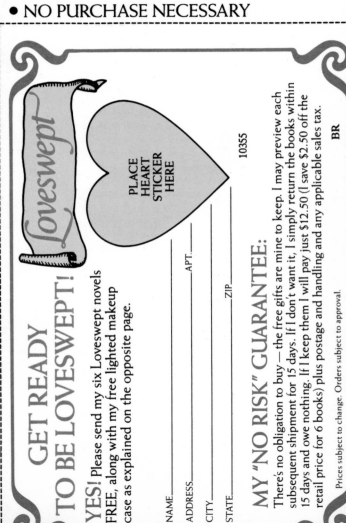

GET READY TO BE LOVESWEPT!

YES! Please send my six Loveswept novels FREE, along with my free lighted makeup case as explained on the opposite page.

Loveswept

PLACE HEART STICKER HERE

NAME _____

ADDRESS _____ APT._____

CITY _____

STATE _____ ZIP_____

10355

MY "NO RISK" GUARANTEE:

There's no obligation to buy — the free gifts are mine to keep. I may preview each subsequent shipment for 15 days. If I don't want it, I simply return the books within 15 days and owe nothing. If I keep them I will pay just $12.50 (I save $2.50 off the retail price for 6 books) plus postage and handling and any applicable sales tax.

BR

Prices subject to change. Orders subject to approval.

REMEMBER!

- The free books and gift are mine to keep!
- There is no obligation!
- I may preview each shipment for 15 days!
- I can cancel anytime!

"That's not the first time you've asked me about being a cop. You want to know how it was? It stank. I was a plain-clothes cop in the narcotics division. My last bust ended with the deaths of two of my best men. That's what it was like being a cop. Satisfied?" He immediately felt guilty for snapping at her, but she was so persistent in bringing up a subject he didn't want to think about, much less discuss.

Ashley realized her mouth was hanging open. Jack was right, she did ask too many questions. But for some reason her curiosity got the best of her every time she was near him. She just had to know what made this strange man tick. "You talk as though it were your fault," Ashley said.

"I was in charge of those men."

The puzzle pieces were beginning to fall into place. "Is that why you shirk responsibility now?" She had gone too far—she could see it in the glassy-eyed look he gave her. Their gazes locked. Ashley realized she was holding her breath.

He stood. "It's time I took you home."

"Jack, don't be angry with me for trying to be your friend," she said, standing.

"I don't want your friendship, lady," he said simply.

He was lashing out at her. Ashley didn't bat an eye. "I don't believe that," she said. "You come across with this gruff, tough-as-nails attitude, but deep down you're human like the rest of us."

"Oh, for Pete's sake! Don't try to analyze me."

"You know I'm right."

"Can I take you home now?"

She stepped closer. "I'm surprised you're able to become intimate with a woman, Jack. Isn't making love rather personal? It means you have to open yourself up to another human being." Once the words were out, there was no taking them back. She had overstepped the boundaries of their relationship, she told herself, and he had every right to be angry. She prepared herself for a good tongue-lashing.

"I don't take sex personally. It's a physical act, plain and simple. *Now*, may I take you home?"

Ashley read the uneasiness in his eyes. "I make you nervous, don't I?"

"I got your number, lady," he said matter-of-factly. "I know your type. You go to bed with a man, and you think you own him. You're real subtle at first, but soon you're inviting him over for dinner and asking him to Sunday picnics at the church. Next thing you know, that man is cutting your grass and painting your house."

"Would you be quiet about painting my house!"

"It's obvious as hell you need a husband and father for your kids."

"And you think I'm so hard up I would consider a burned-out middle-aged hippie for the job?"

"You could do worse."

"I would have to search long and hard," she said between clenched teeth. She planted her hands on her hips and shook her head in disbelief. "I can't believe your audacity. I wouldn't let you train my dog, much less rear my children."

Jack chuckled. "I see the lady has a temper."

"The pope would lose his temper if he was forced to endure your company for any length of time." She stalked toward the door. "You may take me home now."

When Jack pulled into her driveway a little while later, Ashley opened her door and stepped out. Anger infused her. "How dare you sit idly by and tell me what I need or don't need in my life, Jack Sloan! My happiness does not depend on finding a man. You have sorely underestimated me, mister. And you don't know the first thing about life or human need. You gave up all that a long time ago." Then, with gritted teeth, she slammed the door hard enough to make the car rock on its wheels.

Six

"Look, last night—"

Ashley glanced up from the newspaper she was reading at Jeeter's desk and found Jack towering over her. He looked exhausted with another night's growth of beard on his face, and his clothes were wrinkled and disheveled.

"Whose bed did you just crawl out of?" she asked.

Jack took a seat in a chair directly across from her. "I didn't close my eyes all night."

"Not surprising."

"I've been working on a case."

"Uh-huh." She turned her attention back to the article she was reading.

"Would you listen to me!"

Ashley's head snapped up in surprise at his tone of voice. "You're serious, aren't you?"

"Damn serious. A friend of mine called last night, frantic, worried out of his mind. His newborn son was snatched from his crib late yesterday afternoon."

Ashley's hand flew to her mouth. "Oh, no! I heard about it on the news last night, but the police weren't releasing any names. What kind of person would steal a newborn baby?"

Jack raked his fingers through his hair. "The woman who took him was applying for a job as nanny. While my friend's wife, the baby's mother, was on the telephone in the next room, the woman grabbed the baby and ran to her car. Unfortunately, nobody got a license number. All we know is that it's an older-model station wagon and it's white."

"Do you think she'll hurt the baby?"

Jack shook his head. "I don't think he'll come to any harm. It's just going to be difficult to find him."

"So where do we start looking?"

"Well, the police are investigating hospitals and OB-GYN clinics. They seem to think the baby was taken by a woman who recently lost her own child. Which is a reasonable assumption," he added. "There are a couple of clinics in town that treat indigent families. I thought I'd look into it." He stood and glanced at his wristwatch. "I've already called Jeeter and asked for a couple of days off to work on this case. It's up to you whether you want to work on it with me."

"Of course I want to work on it. I'm a mother, aren't I?"

Jack was already halfway to the door, with Ashley behind him. He glanced over his shoulder. She was wearing those tight jeans again. He wouldn't be able to think straight all day. When he spoke, he sounded resigned. "First I want to run by my place and take a quick shower," he said, "and get out of these clothes. Do you mind?"

Ashley's gaze locked with his briefly. "No, that's fine."

When they arrived at the boardinghouse, Ashley didn't know whether to get out or wait for him in the car. Thankfully, he solved the question for her, suggesting she come in and watch television.

Ashley waited for Jack to unlock the door, then followed him into his room, where he switched on the television set. He motioned toward the small kitchenette. "You can make coffee if you like." He was already unbuttoning his shirt.

Ashley mumbled a reply and hurried into the kitchenette as though the devil himself were after her. She was not going to let the man get to her, she told herself, but her hands trembled as she reached for the coffeepot.

"I'd better show you where I keep the coffee," said Jack, coming into the room. He had discarded his shirt and was bare from the waist up.

Ashley heard her own sharp intake of breath at the sight of those broad, sweeping shoulders, and stepped back in order to give him room. The kitchenette suddenly shrank in size. Stepping right in front of her, Jack reached over her head and opened a cabinet. Ashley was given an undistorted view of his wide, heavily matted chest. His biceps were taut and smooth as his arms flexed. His scent, raw masculinity that had nothing to do with soap or cologne, did a number on her central nervous system so that by the time Jack handed her the can of coffee, she was trembling from head to toe.

"Something wrong?" Jack asked.

Ashley shook her head. "N-no, everything is fine."

Jack studied her for a full minute before he planted

his hands on the countertop on either side of her. His expression was thoughtful. "This is one time I wish I didn't have a case waiting," he said, his gaze lingering on her mouth. He reached up and traced her lips with an index finger.

"Jack—"

"Has anybody ever told you what a nice mouth you have?" he asked. "Especially your bottom lip. I'd like to sink my teeth into it. I wouldn't hurt you though. Sometimes I lie awake at night and think of the things I'd like to do to you."

His voice was low and raspy at her ear as he nibbled an earlobe. His warm breath fanned her inner ear, and she shivered. "Jack, I think—"

He shushed her by placing a finger against her lips. "I think you and I should get together once this case is over. What do you say?"

Get together? Ashley gazed questioningly into his dark eyes as he leaned forward and captured her mouth with his. Two strong arms slipped around her waist, one hand planted at the small of her back and the other on her hips. His fingers kneaded the firm muscles of her derriere and pulled her against him, leaving no doubt in her mind that he wanted her. His tongue forged its way past her lips and mated with her own.

When Jack released her, Ashley was literally gasping. Not only had his kiss robbed her of air, it had turned her brain to mush. That was the only excuse she could give for the giddy, weak-kneed feeling that swept over her.

"I'd better take my shower." Jack was surprised by the husky timber of his voice. He didn't sound like himself. But then, his mind and body were always jolted out of sync when he touched her.

Ashley nodded in agreement. She didn't trust herself to speak at the moment. She almost collapsed in relief when Jack left the room. She saw the coffee can in her hand and thought, To heck with it. She didn't need coffee, she told herself. She needed to feel the cool air on her face.

Ashley hurried out of the room, down the hall, and out the front door, moving as fast as her legs could carry her. She should *never* have let him touch her, she told herself, much less kiss her senseless. He saw her as a desperate woman, a woman in pursuit of a man for herself and a father for her children. At least that's how he'd sounded the night before. It was a slap in the face, a direct insult to the fact that she'd supported her family very well for the past four years and could continue doing so for the rest of her life. Even in her marriage she had been the responsible one. Did Jack see her as a helpless individual? she wondered. And why did she care? She certainly didn't have to prove herself to Jack Sloan. But it *did* matter.

When Ashley returned soon afterward, she found Jack frantically pacing the small front porch of the boardinghouse.

"Where have you been?" he demanded, arms akimbo, showing off a pair of beautifully muscled limbs. Concern was etched on his handsome face.

"I needed air," she said simply.

"This isn't a good neighborhood."

"I'm a big girl."

He relaxed somewhat now that he knew she was okay. His gaze raked over her boldly, and his mouth twitched into a smirk. "A man would have to be blind to miss that fact in those butt-hugging jeans you got on."

"You're the one who suggested I dress like you."

"Yeah, but I never said anything about traipsing through a high-crime neighborhood all alone."

"Don't you think I can take care of myself?" she asked testily.

He nodded slowly, as if choosing his words very carefully. "Under most circumstances, yes. But if a couple of thugs grab you out here by yourself, there's not a damn thing you can do about it." He knew the chances of someone abducting her in broad daylight were slim, but dammit, he worried about her! "Just be careful, okay?"

As Ashley followed Jack to his car, her lips were pressed together in a grim line. He was the only man in the world who could make her feel four years old at times.

"Are you ready to stop for lunch?" Jack asked several hours later.

Ashley nodded. "That's fine with me." She tried not to let her disappointment show. They had been to two clinics, and Jack had questioned the nurses and physicians thoroughly. They'd turned up nothing.

Jack slipped his key into the ignition and started the car. He drove less than a mile before he turned into the parking lot of a fast-food restaurant. A telephone booth sat near the road. Jack parked beside it. "I need to check my messages," he told Ashley.

When Jack returned, he looked excited. "We might have a lead," he said. "I just spoke to my friend, the baby's father. Some guy called him from a psychiatric hospital in the next town and told him he might have some information about the kidnapping."

"Did your friend tell the police?"

Jack shook his head. "He doesn't want to go through the red tape if I can take care of it myself. I'm to meet the man on a bench in front of the hospital in exactly one hour. Still hungry?"

Ashley shook her head. "I'm more interested in what this fellow has to say."

"You and me both." Jack started the car and pulled out onto the main road. Instead of going in the direction of town, he turned onto a southbound interstate. "Don't get your hopes up, Sherlock," he told Ashley with a wry smile. "This could be another wild-goose chase."

"How did the man at the hospital know who to call in the first place?" she asked.

"The police released the names of the family this morning, and have shown a composite drawing of the woman several times on TV. Which is good," he added, "and should generate some action."

They arrived at the hospital with time to spare. Jack led Ashley inside and down a hall, where they found several vending machines. Each of them chose a package of crackers and a soft drink. When they finished eating, they went outside and sat down on a bench to wait.

It was well past the appointed hour when a man dressed in white approached them. "Are you here about the baby?" he asked Jack. In response to Jack's nod the man sat down.

"Who's the woman?" he asked. He looked nervous. Jack didn't hesitate. "My assistant. You can trust her. I understand you have some information for me."

"I can't be caught handing out confidential information," the man told him, his expression wary. "They'll fire me. I have a family."

"You won't be caught," Jack said. "I'll guarantee it. But I may as well warn you, it's just a matter of time before the police show up, and they're going to question everybody who knew the lady."

Ashley followed the exchange between the two men. Jack inspired confidence with his quiet, no-nonsense manner. He handled the situation as though it were an everyday occurrence to find himself caught right in the middle of a kidnapping case. In contrast, her heart was hammering wildly in her chest, and her palms were damp with perspiration. But knowing Jack was in full control of himself was reassuring, and she wasn't surprised when the other man slipped him a piece of paper.

"This lady was here last year and stayed almost six months," he told Jack. "Claimed she was pregnant. She wore real baggy clothes, so it was hard to tell. Every so often she'd grab my hand to make me feel the baby kick. She got a real charge out of feeling the baby kick," he said, then shrugged. "Anyway, when I saw the drawing on TV this morning, I knew it was her."

Ashley realized she'd been holding her breath. She released it, and a rush of hot air escaped her lips. "Did this woman lose her baby?" she asked gently.

The man looked into Ashley's eyes. "You don't understand, ma'am. The lady wasn't pregnant."

"Are you sure?" Jack asked.

"The doctor here examined her twice. I wouldn't

have squealed on her, but it's not fair what she did. Anyway, it won't be long before one of the staff recognizes that drawing."

Jack glanced down at the piece of paper in his hand. "Is this her name and address?"

He nodded. "I don't know if she still lives there or not, but it's the only address I could find on her chart. When I saw that baby's mama crying on TV this morning, I knew I had to call."

"You don't know how much we appreciate this," Ashley told the man.

"Yes, I do," he said. "I have a baby boy at home myself."

When Ashley followed Jack back to his car a few minutes later, she could hardly contain her excitement. She climbed in on her side and waited for him to join her in the front seat. "Well? What do you think?"

Jack shrugged. "I think he's telling the truth, but I'm not sure this is the right woman. It could be that she bears a striking resemblance to the kidnapper. Don't get your hopes up."

"We won't know till we check it out," she said eagerly.

"That's right." Jack started the car and pulled out of the parking lot. A half mile down the road he caught the interstate heading north.

Ashley glanced over at him. "I don't know how you can sit there so calmly," she said. "I'm so excited, I can barely stand it."

Jack regarded her. "I try not to let myself get emotionally involved," he said simply. "That way I don't set myself up for disappointment if things don't work out."

"Are you speaking personally or professionally?"

"Both."

She raised her eyebrows and offered a small smile. "Do you have any other words of wisdom you'd like to impart this afternoon?"

He looked over at her and grinned. "Don't take responsibility for anything or anyone, and you won't get into trouble."

Ashley shook her head. "I don't know how you can go through life so detached," she said. "I would imagine you'd get lonely."

"I prefer being alone."

"It's not a weak thing to need other people." Ashley could tell she was wasting her breath—Jack wasn't listening.

Jack slowed and exited the interstate. He drove for another ten minutes before he pulled the piece of paper from his pocket.

"Are we close?" Ashley asked.

Jack nodded and turned onto a side road. They counted the house numbers and pulled in in front of a house bearing the same address as that on the slip of paper he held. "Wait in the car," he said. "This won't take long."

Ashley watched him make his way to the house in long strides. When he rang the doorbell, a man answered. They talked for several minutes before Jack knocked on the neighbors' doors and spoke with them. When Jack returned to the car, he was frowning.

"What happened?" Ashley asked.

"Just as I thought. She moved away. One of the neighbors remembered she used to work at a doughnut shop downtown."

"Which one?"

"She didn't know."

"But there's no telling how many doughnut shops there are downtown."

His expression was weary. "Exactly."

Ashley sighed. Why she had ever imagined investigative work was exciting was beyond her. So far it had proved to be an endless amount of legwork, dead ends, and frustration. Still, she was determined to see it through to the end. "I think I'd better call Chip and tell him I'm going to be late," she said. "Also, I need to check on Mikie."

Jack glanced at his wristwatch. "I didn't realize it was so late. Why don't I drop you off at the agency, so you can pick up your car and go home?"

"That's all the way back across town. Just let me make a telephone call."

Once Ashley had called home, they proceeded down the long list of doughnut shops from the Yellow Pages that Jack had ripped out of a telephone book. It was late when Jack exited one of the many doughnut shops they'd visited that day with a sack of glazed doughnuts and two cups of coffee. When Ashley saw the look on his face, she scratched the shop off the list.

Jack took a bite of his doughnut, swallowed, and followed it with a swig of coffee. "How many doughnut shops do we have left?"

Ashley glanced at her list. "About a zillion."

He chuckled. "Getting tired, Sherlock?"

She craned her neck to one side and massaged a sore muscle. "I've been sitting in this spot for so long, I think my body has grown roots."

"I wish I had a cigarette."

"No, you don't. You're doing too good to start smoking again. Try to think of something else."

The all-encompassing look he gave her left no doubt about the direction his thoughts had taken. A slow, sensual grin broke out on his face. "Either one makes me itch just to think about it." He laughed when Ashley looked away in embarrassment.

Jack reached for the Yellow Pages and scanned the listings of doughnut shops. He drained his coffee cup. "Ready?" he asked, starting the car. When Ashley nodded, he put the car into gear and drove away.

Fifteen minutes later, Jack pulled into the parking lot of yet another doughnut shop, one that looked very much the same as the others. He sighed heavily, got out of the car, and closed the door. He went inside, stood beside the cash register, and waited for the manager.

Ashley stared at Jack as he spoke to a man and pulled out the drawing of the mystery lady. She was exhausted. She couldn't help but wonder what progress the police had made. She wrinkled her brow thoughtfully as she watched Jack follow the man to another part of the building.

When Jack returned, he was grinning. It was obvious he was onto something. He opened his door and got in—then, without warning, pulled Ashley into his arms for a loud kiss. When he released her, she was staring dumbly at him.

"Bingo!" He held up the sheet of paper. "The manager recognized her as a former employee. Gave me her mother's address."

"Yes, but how do you know her mother still lives here?"

"I called."

"You called? What did you say?"

"I asked her if she was interested in buying vinyl siding for her house." When she rolled her eyes at him, he shrugged. "It was the first thing that came to mind."

He reached forward and turned on the ignition. "I know you're going to think this is crazy, but I could have sworn I heard a baby cry in the background while I was talking to her." He glanced over at her. "You know how you wish for something to happen so badly that you finally imagine it?"

"Maybe you really did hear a baby cry."

"Naw, that would be too easy. Two things I've learned in this job are, never get your hopes up and never expect things to be simple."

Jack turned onto a dark street some time later. The mood was tense, and neither of them had said much on the drive over. "Okay, this is it," he said, his voice deadly serious. "Look for five-one-seven. Damn, why don't these people keep their porch lights on? Okay, there's five-one-five."

"This is it," Ashley said, motioning to a small frame house. "Five-one-seven," she read aloud from the mailbox.

"Look at that." Jack pointed to the driveway. In it sat a white station wagon.

"What do we do now?" Ashley whispered, her heart thumping wildly in her chest.

"I'm going to sit right here and make sure nobody leaves," he told her. "I want you to go to the house across the street and call the police. Tell them I sent you, and that I said to bring a search warrant."

•   •   •

"I think this calls for a celebration," Jack said more than two hours later, smiling at the scene before him. Several police cars were still parked in the yard and along the street, even though the woman responsible for the brouhaha had been taken away.

Ashley couldn't stop grinning. She was almost giddy with excitement. "I still don't believe it. Thank God it all came out right, and the baby is fine. And my children are going to see us on TV. I just don't believe it."

Jack started the car and drove away, hoping to sneak off before yet another microphone and camera were thrust in his face. He was certain he and Ashley had been asked more questions than the kidnapper.

"I'd love to see the expression on the parents' faces when they get their baby back," she said wistfully. Although the baby had seemed in good shape when the police had taken him from the woman's arms, he had been whisked away in an ambulance and taken to the nearest hospital, where he would be examined and handed over to his relieved parents.

"I'm sure it will be on the eleven o'clock news," Jack said. "If we hurry, we can make it to my place in time to watch it. It just so happens I have a bottle of champagne in my refrigerator. You can't have a celebration without champagne."

When they arrived at Jack's place, Ashley headed straight for the telephone and called Chip. She filled him in on the events and told him to watch the news. "I'll be home in a little while," she said. "Don't bother waiting up for me." She hung up the telephone and accepted the cup Jack handed her.

"When's the last time you drank champagne out of a coffee cup?" he asked.

Ashley smiled and took a sip of the bubbly liquid. "Chip's going to record the news on the VCR, so Mikie can watch it in the morning."

"Sit down." Jack motioned for her to take a seat on the bed while he turned on the television set.

"I probably won't sleep all night," she said, feeling keyed up after the events of the day. "All that driving was worth it after all, wasn't it? Now, I don't mind all those hours we spent searching."

Jack glanced up from the television. "You think it took us a long time to find the baby?" he asked in disbelief. "We only worked one day on the case. We could have searched for days, even weeks. This kind of thing doesn't happen often. We got lucky."

"You're right," she said. "I'm just excited. Those policemen, not to mention the FBI, treated you like a hero."

"They'll forget about it soon enough."

"Yes, but the baby's parents won't," she said. "They'll remember you for the rest of their lives."

"Let's not make a big deal out of it, okay? It was just another job."

Ashley looked surprised. "Jack, how can you say that? A baby's life was at stake here."

"The baby wasn't harmed, and I seriously doubt the woman would have hurt him."

"What do you think will happen to her?"

He shrugged. "Who knows? The D.A. will have to take into account that she spent time in a psychiatric hospital."

Ashley glanced at the TV. "Quick, turn up the sound, the news is on!"

Jack turned up the volume on the television set and refilled their cups before he took a seat on the bed next to Ashley. She was literally bursting at the seams with excitement, and wasn't aware she was clinging to his arm. Jack was acutely aware of her touch.

"Did you hear that?" she asked, once the news had flashed a short interview with the baby's parents. "They called us miracle workers!"

"Yeah, I heard." He was tired of thinking about the baby. He had thought of little else all day. It had been hell trying to concentrate on the case with Ashley sitting only inches from him in the car. He stood, reached toward the television set, and turned it off.

"What did you do that for?"

"Because I want to think about you right now. About us."

She sucked in her breath. "Us?"

"Remember when I told you I wanted us to get together when the case was over?"

Ashley swallowed hard. "Uh-huh."

"It's over."

She stared at him a full minute before she said anything. "Do we have any more champagne?"

Jack gave her a rueful smile and took her cup. "We're all out. We're also out of reasons to avoid this conversation." He reclaimed his seat on the bed beside her.

Ashley realized she was breathing fast. Lord, she would probably hyperventilate. Perhaps she should ask for a small paper sack. She was prevented from doing so when the telephone rang.

Jack did not miss the look of relief on Ashley's face, nor did he miss her look of disbelief when he merely leaned over and unplugged the phone from the wall.

"What if it's important?"

"Nothing is that important." When she glanced away, he placed an index finger beneath her chin and turned her face so she was looking directly into his eyes. She was no good at this kind of thing, she wanted to tell him. He leaned close, and very gently placed a kiss on her chin.

"Do that thing you do with your dimple," he said.

She blinked. "Huh?"

"Smile."

She forced herself to smile despite the case of nerves that had taken over her body.

"Bingo." He leaned over and kissed the irresistible cleft next to her mouth. He kissed the tip of her nose, and when she closed her eyes briefly, he kissed each eyelid. Then he lowered his mouth to hers. Her lips were pliant and sweet, and felt so very right against his own.

The kiss deepened as Jack slowly and very gently lowered her onto the bed. When his tongue found its way into her mouth, her own tongue met it eagerly. He teased and tantalized it until Ashley snaked her arms around his neck.

Jack raised his head slightly, so that his lips barely brushed hers when he spoke. "I can't believe how lucky I am to have you in my arms," he said softly. He recaptured her lips before she could say anything more.

Ashley's heart fluttered wildly in her chest as Jack continued his sensual assault on her lips. He nibbled her bottom lip with his teeth before soothing it with his tongue.

Jack knew he had never tasted anything sweeter than Ashley's mouth. It was like dipping into a honey pot. He couldn't get enough of her. Even as she lay beneath him yieldingly, he wanted more. He wanted to hold her naked in his arms, lave her breasts with his tongue, and know the ecstasy of filling her with himself. The mere thought made him crazy.

Ashley felt her control slipping away with every breath she drew. She had heard someone say once that the stomach was the seat of emotions. Now, she knew it was the truth: Her stomach had not stopped fluttering since Jack had taken her in his arms. His skillful tongue prodded her lips open once more in yet another exploration of her mouth. She tightened her arms around his neck, aching for him even though his hard body was already pressing deliciously into hers. She slid her hands across his shoulders and down his back, delighting in the feel of his hard muscles.

Jack broke the kiss and repositioned himself so that Ashley wasn't bearing the brunt of his weight. The taste and touch and smell of her set his body on fire. What had started out on his part as a few stolen kisses had ignited a flame low in his belly that couldn't be ignored. His mouth took hers again, roughly, hungrily, and their tongues reunited.

Ashley moaned softly as Jack pressed his body intimately against hers. She arched against him, knowing all the while they had pushed themselves past the limits of self-control. She wanted him. She had wanted him from the beginning, she admitted to herself. But he was wild and reckless, everything she was not. They were direct opposites of each other. They were . . . Oh, damn, she couldn't think. She closed her eyes. Where had logical thought flown to? she wondered. Where had this foolhardy, devil-may-care abandonment come from?

Jack's gaze locked with hers. His fingers fumbled with the buttons on her blouse. He sought for any signs of disapproval in her eyes, but found no traces. Instead, they were soft with invitation. He kissed each spot he bared, fingering the wispy lace of her bra when it came into view and kissing the gentle swells that rose above each cup. When at last he had removed both her blouse and bra, he gazed down appreciatively at her perfect breasts. Nothing short of death could have prevented him from taking one rosy crest between his lips.

Ashley sucked in her breath sharply as Jack cupped both breasts in his palms. toying first with one nipple, then the other. The sensation sent a rush of heat through her body, congregating at the base of her thighs. One hand sought the fastening of her slacks. Ashley stiffened in response, common sense and logic warring with her thoughts and emotions. But despite what her mind was telling her, it felt so *right* being in Jack's arms. It was like coming home to a place she'd always known existed in the back of her mind but had wondered if she would ever find. It was like discovering the pot of gold at the end of the rainbow.

Their bodies, it seemed to Ashley, had been designed specifically for each other. They were like human puzzle pieces; each feminine curve was complemented by the hard planes and unique hollows of his body. At his gentle prodding she lifted her hips from the bed so he could pull away her slacks. He dropped them onto the floor, and her panties followed. Jack gazed down at her adoringly.

"You're beautiful," he said, his voice a husky purr.

It took every bit of willpower she could muster to lie there and not scramble beneath the covers. She smiled shyly. "You sound surprised."

He nodded. "I thought women who had babies got stretch marks and all that stuff." His eyes took inventory as he spoke.

"I guess I got lucky, huh?"

He gave her a slow, sensual grin. "I'm the one who got lucky, Sherlock." Once again his lips captured hers. One hand moved to the inside of her thighs and stroked her incredibly smooth skin. Her legs were long and shapely and slightly tan. Even her feet were pretty, slim and delicate, her toenails the color of ripe plums. When he dipped his fingers into the honeyed crevice at the base of her thighs, he thought he would lose control. His hand cupped the silken black curls there while his fingers acquainted themselves with her flesh. He stroked the very crux of her desire until she cooed with pleasure. An undeniable ache consumed her, and she could think of nothing but abating it.

Jack moved away from her long enough to shrug out of his own clothes. When he returned, he was naked and hard for her. Ashley gazed longingly at his strong, hair-roughened body. He was lean, the muscles in his thighs and stomach taut but smooth. A thatch of dark curls nestled around his hardness. Ashley held out her arms to receive him.

His lips devoured hers as he sank into her. In all of his life he had never known such exquisite pleasure. She was so perfect for him, and he was lost to her, to the sheath of muscles that gripped him so tightly. He mentally cursed those same muscles for stealing his restraint. But with Ashley there was no holding back.

Ashley slipped her arms around Jack's waist as she met each measured thrust. She dropped her hands to his firm hips and felt the muscles contract with each plunge. His own hands returned to her breasts, the gentle coaxing replaced by a more determined touch.

Ashley closed her eyes, all self-control lost to the man moving over her. A delicious white heat pulsed low in her belly and thighs, and exploded in a million tiny starbursts, sending her over the edge and robbing her of coherent thought. Jack's breath was hot in her ear as he rasped out her name and shuddered in her arms.

Some time later, Jack opened his eyes and gazed down at the sleeping woman snuggled in the crook of his arms. He watched her for a moment, thinking he should probably wake her. It was late.

It's later than you think, Jack, a voice told him. You've made love with her, and now you're going to have to face the consequences, take responsibility for what you've done. Damn, why had he made love with her? he suddenly asked himself. Better yet, why had he made love with her twice? Already his body was beginning to stir in response to the naked figure pressed against him and the shapely thigh placed intimately between his own.

Another thought hit him. How in the hell was he

going to work with her now? If it had been difficult before, it would be doubly so now, and he would worry about her safety even more. And how would he keep his mind on his work when every time he looked at her, he'd think of her naked and lying beneath him?

Yet despite all this, he knew he no longer wanted to be rid of her. Suddenly, she had become very important to him, and he didn't want to lose her—ever.

Seven

It was late the following morning when Ashley stumbled into the kitchen in search of a cup of coffee. Chip came in right behind her. She was thankful Jack had told her to come in at noon so she could catch up on her sleep. She blushed for the umpteenth time as she remembered why she'd been out so late the night before.

"Good morning, Chip," she said pleasantly, giving him a sleepy smile.

"Mornin'."

"Something wrong?" She would have been deaf and blind not to notice his gruff tone, or the way he kept his back to her.

He faced her. "I waited up for you last night. Till two in the morning," he added.

This time Ashley blushed all the way from the base of her neck to the tops of her ears. "I'm sorry I was late," she said, "but I was so keyed up after finding that baby . . . Jack and I sort of celebrated afterward. I told you not to wait up for me," she reminded him gently.

"I always wait up for you, just as you wait up for me. Only you don't usually come in so late."

"Chip—"

"And I don't like that Harley Davidson guy anyway."

"His name isn't Harley, it's Jack. Jack Sloan."

Chip shook his head. "I don't like him."

"Why not?"

"Because he's rough-looking, that's why. I want you to date, Mother, but do you have to go out with a man who has more stubble on his face than Don Johnson?"

Ashley didn't quite know what to say. It was the first time Chip had ever voiced a complaint about a man she was seeing. Not that she was really seeing Jack. "I'm sorry you feel that way, Chip," she said, "but I work with Mr. Sloan, and he's really very decent." Her words surprised even her.

Chip wasn't convinced. "I know you have to work with him, but that doesn't mean you have to spend every waking moment together." Without another word, he stalked out of the room.

Ashley felt like a fool. She only prayed Chip didn't suspect how far her relationship with Jack had gone. There was no condoning the fact that she'd hopped into bed with a man she'd known two weeks. What had happened to the levelheaded woman she'd once been? she wondered. The same woman who'd set high standards for herself as well as her children. Had common sense flown out the window?

Ashley was bursting at the seams with guilt by the time she arrived at the office two hours later. She couldn't quite meet Jack's eyes. She was thankful Jeeter was present and was more interested in the kidnapping case than in her or Jack. She had to concentrate in order to keep up with the questions he fired at her.

Finally, Jeeter stood and hiked his pants up over his belly. "Well, I promised a buddy I'd meet him for lunch," he said.

When Jeeter left, Ashley let out a sigh of relief. But the air had no sooner escaped her lungs than she felt Jack's arms slip around her waist possessively. It startled her so badly, her heart lurched in her chest. He turned her around slowly to face him. "I didn't get a damn bit of sleep last night after I drove you here for your car."

She squirmed free. "Jack, about last night . . ."

He grinned. "I thought it was great between us, Sherlock. What about you?"

"It never should have happened," she said. "I don't know what got into me, but I've never . . . ever—"

Jack put a hand on either side of her shoulders. "I see you've already started the ol' guilt process. Why can't you just accept it for what it was?"

"And exactly what was it?"

"A damn good time, that's what." He gave her a wicked grin. "At least you *looked* as though you were having a good time." There, he'd said it, just as he'd planned. He was making it crystal clear from the beginning that he didn't expect a serious relationship to evolve from their encounter. He wanted to set guidelines and limitations. He wanted to keep it simple—he had to.

"My son was angry with me for coming in as late as I did."

"He'll get over it. He frowned when she pulled away. "Look, baby—"

"Don't call me that," she said tersely. "Not ever."

Jack held up both hands as though surrendering. "I didn't mean anything by it." The lady was in a rotten mood, he told himself. Better proceed cautiously. "Listen, the boy is probably just upset because you're spending time with someone other than his father. That's completely normal."

Ashley regarded him. He spoke like a professional, but she'd be willing to bet he'd never known a teenager in his life. She shook her head. "You don't understand. Chip never gives me any trouble. He's been the man of the house since the day his father moved out. He works part time just to buy his clothes and school supplies, so I won't have to fork out the money. He's always on the honor roll. He's mature and levelheaded, and I don't know what I would do without him."

Jack pondered the thought. "I resented having to help my family," he confessed. "It ticked me off that I couldn't go on to college like the rest of my friends— not that my grades were particularly good. But instead, I had to work two jobs to pay the bills, just because my lazy, good-for-nothing old man up and left us. I was the happiest man in the world the day my mother remarried and set me free."

"I'm sure the responsibility was overwhelming."

"Damn right."

"But Chip insisted on helping right from the start," she said. "And frankly, I think it's good for him to work and learn how to budget his money. Builds character. I know I expect a lot from him, but that's because I don't want him to turn out like his father. My ex-husband was pampered by his parents for so long that he couldn't cope with a wife and children. It was too much for him." She paused. "Anyway, you have to understand that Chip and I have a different sort of relationship. We're not just mother and son. We're friends, good buddies."

"If you're friends like you say you are, then he'll understand that you're a normal healthy woman with needs."

"We're getting off the subject," she said. "This is really between you and me, and has nothing to do with my son. I was raised with old-fashioned values, and I can't toss them aside that easily."

"Okay, what do you want? Do you want to be wined and dined first? I can do that."

She blushed. "I never said that. I merely feel two people should get to know each other before they become intimate."

"So where do you want to go for dinner tonight?" he asked, shifting to a cocky stance. He should have seen it coming, he told himself. A woman like Ashley would never be satisfied with a relationship based solely on sex. She would insist on compatibility in other areas as well. The funny thing was, he was beginning to feel the same way.

"I'm having dinner at home tonight, since I was out so late last night."

"Dinner at your place? That's fine with me."

Ashley didn't have the heart to tell him she had planned on having dinner alone with her children. And she had no idea how Chip would react. Not only that, she was not about to start making demands on Jack. He would convince himself she was after him, out to get a man.

"You don't *have* to come, you know."

"I want to. Very much," he added. It was the truth. "I'll even bring dessert."

"Is seven-thirty okay?"

He nodded, already looking forward to it.

The day dragged for Ashley. Although Jack didn't refer to the previous night again, and remained polite and professional through the day, she could not put the events out of her mind. Every time she met his gaze, she was reminded of those same dark eyes searing into hers as he'd made love to her. It had been a delicious, sensational experience, one she'd not likely forget. And it wasn't over yet. He was having dinner at her house tonight. That could only mean he hoped to carry on their present relationship, one that she wasn't capable of continuing. Jack Sloan would make mincemeat out of her heart, and she wasn't taking any chances.

When Ashley and Jack returned to the office at the end of the day, they found a large balloon arrangement waiting for them, a gift from the parents of the baby boy they'd rescued the day before.

Jeeter beamed proudly at them. "Channel Six News has been looking for you two. They've been by here twice."

"I'm leaving before they come back," Ashley said, picking up her purse.

Jack stood as well. "Me too. I don't feel like answering a bunch of questions tonight."

"What should I tell them when they come back?" Jeeter asked.

"Tell them we were just doing our job."

Ashley walked out the front door with Jack on her heels. "Are you sure you don't want to drop by my place first?" he asked.

She didn't have to look in his eyes to catch his meaning. "I can't, Jack," she said, knowing he would never understand. How could a man like Jack understand things like children and obligations? She walked to her car, feeling his gaze on her. The car was stifling inside after sitting in the sun all day. She started it and flipped on the air conditioner, watching from her rearview mirror as Jack got into his own car. How tempting it was to follow him, she thought, to lie in his arms and bask in the warmth of his body. To know the pain of too much pleasure.

Ashley trembled from head to toe as she tried to maneuver her car out of the parking lot and onto the main road.

When Ashley arrived home, she found Chip and his girlfriend watching television, and Mikie playing in the backyard with a friend. Chip was dressed for work, wearing dark pants and a shirt and tie.

"I have to go in early tonight," he told her once Ashley had spoken to the girl beside him. "One of the guys is out sick."

Ashley sighed her relief. That meant Chip wouldn't be home when Jack arrived for dinner. That was one obstacle she didn't feel like facing tonight after having missed so much sleep the night before. She had been so tense all day, not to mention exhausted, and she wished she could just climb into bed. "I'll make you a sandwich," she told him, already heading for the kitchen.

He stood, as did the girl beside him. "Don't bother, I've already eaten."

"Then I'll drive you to work."

"Jill's giving me a lift," he said, grinning at his girlfriend. They headed for the front door. Chip glanced over his shoulder at Ashley. "See you later."

Ashley shrugged to herself, then went out to speak to her younger son and his friend. Once she'd said hello, she went inside and prepared the casserole she'd planned for dinner, shoved it in the oven, and straightened the house.

By the time seven-thirty rolled around, Ashley was a bundle of nerves. Mikie had come into the kitchen several times looking for something to eat, and it was all she could do to make him wait. It was something they went through every night, a ritual, and Ashley had come to expect it. "You may have one slice of cheese and that's all," she told the boy firmly. She was almost thankful when the doorbell rang.

Ashley would not have recognized Jack had she not known he was coming. She unlocked the door and let him pass through while she did a double take. Gone were the worn jeans and T-shirt he always wore, replaced by a pair of gray slacks and a gray and white pullover. "You look nice," she said, surprise ringing loud in her voice. She was so stunned by his appearance that she didn't notice the bouquet of flowers or the covered dish he held.

"These are for you," he said, thankful when she

had taken them. He'd never bought a woman flowers before, and it was the last time he planned on doing so. Not only had most of the petals fallen off in the front seat of his car, he felt dumb walking around with a fistful of stems. Normal men did not traipse all over town carrying daisies and pansies and . . . aw, hell, he didn't know what kind of flowers they were.

Ashley was clearly impressed, and a bit stunned by the flowers. "Thank you," she said. She accepted the covered dish with raised brows.

"Its a strawberry cheesecake," he said. "I stopped by a bakery on the way over."

"You bought an *entire* cheesecake?"

"Uh-huh."

Ashley tried to mentally calculate how much it had cost him. Her hamburg-and-macaroni casserole would look weak in comparison. She was still shaking her head as she led him into the kitchen, where she had been preparing a tossed salad. She carried it to the table, stopping by the refrigerator for a bottle of Italian dressing.

"Go ahead and sit down," she said, motioning for him to take a seat. "I'll get Mikie." She returned a few minutes later. "He's sound asleep on the couch and won't budge."

Jack didn't look the least bit disappointed. "Guess that means we eat alone, huh?"

Ashley seated herself across the table from Jack, wishing she had stopped by the store for a bottle of wine. She could use a drink right now, she told herself. Anything to relax. Her usual hot bath was out of the question. "Salad?" she asked, holding the bowl out for him.

"After you."

This was not the Jack Sloan she knew, she told herself. This man was polite and well-dressed and mannerly. The Jack she knew dressed like a hobo, and his manners were sorely lacking. Ashley took some salad for herself, then passed the bowl to Jack. Was it an attempt to woo her back into his bed? she wondered. Probably. Jack would stop at nothing to get what he wanted. Still, he'd been warm and loving in bed; he wasn't the rascal he appeared to be in his day-to-day existence. She could very well fall in love with the man who'd shared his tender side with her the night before. That thought startled her. She gazed at Jack as though seeing him for the first time. When he caught her staring, he gave her a slow, intimate smile.

"You know, I was thinking," he finally said. "Why don't I buy some ribs this weekend and barbecue them over here?"

"You want to have a cookout?"

"If you have a grill."

"Sure I do, but—" She paused. "Chip and I are going to start painting the house this weekend," she said, knowing that would change his mind entirely. "I've put it off as long as I can. Could we have the cookout another time?"

He shrugged. "It was just an idea." She was probably waiting for him to offer to help paint the house, he told himself, unaccustomed to being turned down by a woman.

"This is very good," he said a few minutes later, when he'd taken a bite of the casserole.

She smiled. "Thanks. I don't do a lot of cooking during the week."

"I don't do much cooking ever," he confessed. "If I can't eat it out of a can, I don't buy it."

"Do you eat out often?"

He nodded. "I know this waitress at Sadie's Kitchen, and I call every day to find out what's on special. If it's something I like, I go. If not, I open a can. I bought myself a small microwave so I wouldn't have to use the stove. I figure, why go to all that trouble just for one person?"

"Don't you ever get tired of being alone?" she asked. "I would go crazy if I didn't have Chip and Mikie around."

He arched one brow. "What gave you the idea that I spent so much time alone?"

Ashley blushed. "I just assumed . . . oh, never mind."

Jack chuckled. "I'm willing to bet you're the last woman on earth who still blushes or insists on making love in the dark."

"Jack—"

"Loosen up, Ash. You're supposed to be a woman of the nineties."

"I don't see how you can say that after last night," she said, her annoyance growing. "After all, we've only known each other two weeks."

"Time doesn't mean a damn thing. It's what you feel inside that counts. It takes some people months or years to realize they've got a good thing. We were lucky it happened right away for us. I wanted you from the start. As a matter of fact, I want you right now."

Ashley jumped up from the table and grabbed his empty plate. "I'll get you a slice of cheesecake," she said quickly. She hurried across the kitchen with the dirty plates and stuck them in the sink. She pulled the cheesecake out of the refrigerator and sliced it. Once she had put slices on two small plates, she carried them to the table and placed one in front of Jack. She'd started for her own chair when Jack suddenly stood and closed his fingers around her wrist. She looked up in question.

"What's wrong with you tonight?" he asked, taking the saucer from her and setting it on the table. He anchored his free hand around her waist. "You're all strung out. I feel like if I kiss you like I've been dying to do all evening, you'll shatter into a million pieces. What gives?"

Ashley forced herself to meet his gaze. "It's about last night. It was a mistake, and now I feel terribly uncomfortable around you."

"That's the second time you've said that. *Why* was it a mistake?"

"Because . . ."

"Didn't you enjoy it?"

Her heart leaped to her throat. "Of course I enjoyed it."

"Are you going to deny that it was good between us? Or very possibly the best?"

"I don't make comparisons."

"Well, I do."

She blushed. "You and I are just too different. A relationship between us would be a disaster."

Jack sighed and raked his fingers through his hair. He had no idea how endearing she found the simple gesture. It left his hair slightly tousled and very sexy.

"Why do we have to make a big deal out of this?" he insisted. "Why does it even have to become a relationship in the first place? Why do we have to attach labels to everything we do? Why do we have to feel guilty for merely taking some of life's little pleasures?" He began to pace. "And why, for heaven's sake, can't you accept me for who I am?"

"Which is?"

"Just me," he said, stabbing a finger at his chest. "I don't *want* to be poured into the same old mold as everybody else. I don't *want* a house and a two-car garage or a passel of kids. I don't *want* to live with some woman who nags day and night—"

"I haven't asked you to."

"—and wears that white gunk on her face when she goes to bed, so that before too long a man can't help but wonder why sex was invented."

Ashley didn't know how to respond. Somehow, the conversation had shifted from emphasizing their differences to making commitments. Perhaps they were one and the same, she mused. Obviously, Jack wasn't prepared to offer her anything more than a good romp in the sack, while she, on the other hand, needed emotional support as well.

But she was in too deep with him now to let go. By allowing him to make love to her, she had sealed her fate, and she would make whatever compromises she must in order to be with him. She wouldn't think about what she was giving up, her own emotional needs. She wouldn't think of how uncomfortable it would be working with him or what Chip might say. She would take whatever Jack could offer her for the time being. A piece of his heart was better than none at all. Besides, the decision had already been made for her. She had fallen in love with him.

Eight

Jack watched the play of emotions on Ashley's face and wondered what she could be thinking. She probably was thinking of a way to get rid of him, he thought, especially after the things he'd said. But he'd had to be honest with her. While he cared for her and enjoyed being with her, he just couldn't handle a deep, meaningful relationship. He was not husband or father material, and the sooner she realized that, the sooner they could proceed. *If* she still wanted to. The sad, almost resigned look on her face suggested she did not.

"I'd better go," he said softly.

"You don't have to rush off," Ashley said. She wanted him to stay. Heaven help her, but she enjoyed being with him, despite their differences. Perhaps it had a lot to do with her attraction to him, she thought. Jack was so unlike anyone she'd ever known, a maverick, that's what he was, but she felt herself being drawn to him like a sailor to the sea.

He was the only man who could raise her dander one minute and kiss her until she was weak-kneed and breathless the next. In his arms she had felt beautiful and treasured. It had felt good to be alive. "Besides, I have to wait up for Chip. He usually doesn't get home until eleven."

"Then let me help you wash the dishes," he offered. Jack was already at work, clearing the kitchen table. "I think we ought to call it an early night though," he said. "We didn't get a whole lot of sleep last night." He didn't have to look at her to know she was blushing. He picked up their dessert plates. "What d'you say we eat this after we clean the kitchen?" When Ashley nodded, he set them on the counter.

Once the kitchen was clean, Ashley suggested they carry their desert out to the picnic table. Instead of taking a seat directly across from Ashley, Jack scooted in right beside her. She was very much aware of his right thigh pressing against hers.

They ate in silence. Finally, Jack pushed his plate aside and turned toward her, straddling the bench in order to see her better. The air was thick with tension. He had to talk to her, get some things out in the open. He had learned a long time ago that people *had* to communicate. But he'd never been good with words, and, more often than not, his mouth got him into trouble. The fact was, he was so confused about his feelings toward her and what to do about them that he felt scared for the first time in his life. He had never considered himself a coward. Heck, he'd been in more messes than ten people would face in a lifetime. But Ashley scared the living daylights out of him because she brought out emotions that he hadn't known existed. The un-known was frightening.

"I know you think I don't have any feelings," he finally said, mustering every bit of courage he could find, "but I want you to know last night meant a helluva lot to me. In fact, I've thought of little else."

Ashley stared at Jack for a full minute before she said anything. The man had done it again. Just when she thought she was beginning to understand him, he did an about-face. One moment he was pulling away from her with all his might, and the next thing she knew he was opening himself up to her, exposing a man who was . . . yes, almost vul-nerable. Trying to keep up with him made her head spin. But it was times like these, with him sitting there gazing at her in the moonlight with that ten-der expression, that she felt like throwing her arms around him and never letting go. "I don't really know you at all," she finally said.

"Then we're even. I'm not sure I know myself ei-ther. And you're not making it any easier on me."

She was confused. "What have I done?"

"You've made me crazy, that's what you've done." When she continued to look baffled, he grinned and tweaked her nose playfully. Actually, it was what she *hadn't* done that kept him in a state of bewilder-ment. She wasn't making demands on him, and that was most confusing, considering her makeup. If she had become demanding and insisted on some sort of commitment from him, he could have just walked out, despite his desire to be with her. It would have been so much simpler. As it was, he was left up to his own devices, and he wasn't so sure that was a good idea.

Jack scooted closer and turned her around so that she was leaning against him, her elbows anchored on his thighs. He snaked his arms around her waist, then nuzzled his face against the downy softness at the nape of her neck. Chills danced along her spine.

"You want to know one of the things I like best about you?" he asked. He didn't wait for her answer. "Your skin. It's as soft as a baby's skin. Has anybody ever told you that? Dumb question, of course they have." He squirmed on the bench.

"Am I hurting you?" she asked, twisting her head around to see him.

"Yes, you're hurting me, but not the way you think. It's just your backbone is pressed against my . . . against a very delicate area." He repositioned himself. "There, that's better. Perhaps I'll be able to father children after all."

Ashley laughed softly. "We certainly wouldn't want to keep those wonderful genes of yours from sprouting up in future generations, would we?"

"True." He leaned forward and nibbled the back of her ear. She shivered. "Cold?"

She didn't have to turn around to know he was grinning from ear to ear. "Of course I'm not cold, and you know it."

He chuckled. "Okay, you can turn around now. As much as I enjoy kissing your neck, I prefer your face."

Ashley stood and turned around on the bench. "Is this okay?"

"Perfect." Jack placed an open palm on either side of her face and leaned forward, brushing his lips lightly against hers. He raised his head a fraction and looked into her eyes before capturing her lips in a slow, leisurely kiss. He slipped his arms around her waist and drew her nearer.

Ashley's mind reeled as the kiss deepened. Jack's tongue was everywhere, flitting like a butterfly, touching and tasting the sweetness of her mouth. One hand at the small of her back massaged her and pulled her closer. His chest was big and wide, his stomach firm, and his thigh muscles hard and taut, a contrast to his gentle touch.

Jack's lips never stilled, even as he raised his hands to her lush breasts and covered them with an open palm. They were femininely soft, high and firm. He could feel her nipples through her bra. He had discovered how ultrasensitive they were. He only had to stroke them to turn them into erect nubs.

Jack broke the kiss and sucked in a deep, shuddering breath. Unless she was planning to invite him into her bedroom, which he knew she wasn't, he had to put on the brakes. He couldn't kiss her without wanting to make love to her. Damn. He was literally aching for her. But it was different somehow from what he had wanted from women in the past.

It wasn't just sex. He had ample opportunity for good, rowdy sex. It was what came afterward. With most women, he wanted to disappear as soon as it was over, and a lot of women seemed content for him to do just that. His ex-wife had been no different.

It wasn't like that with Ashley. After they had made love, she had stretched and cuddled up to him like a kitten to a potbellied stove in winter. He had not wanted her to leave. He enjoyed holding her, stroking that thick dark mane of hers and inhaling her essence. As silly as it seemed, he had wanted to tell

er things about himself. Dumb things. Like the
ime in third grade when he threw up onstage while
eciting a Christmas poem to an audience of par-
nts and teachers. He'd loved Amy Louise Washing-
on at the time, and she had loved him. Until that
lay when he'd lost his lunch on her new black patent-
eather shoes in front of the entire school. And what
bout the time he'd been elected captain of the safety
atrol squad in sixth grade? He had never consid-
red these events important in his life until he met
shley. She would think they were important.

"Something wrong?" Ashley asked when he pulled
way abruptly.

He stood, thankful it was dark and she couldn't
ee his rather blatant state of arousal. "I think it's
ime for me to go. Besides, you need to catch up on
our sleep."

She nodded. Her hands trembled as she picked up
heir plates and carried them into the house with
Jack on her heels. She barely had time to set them
n the sink before he turned her around and pulled
ier into his arms once more.

He gazed at her for a moment, drinking in the
sight of her. He hated leaving her even for a minute.
f he knew the right words, he would tell her how
oretty she was. How could he describe a sunrise? he
vondered, because her face reminded him of one
vhen she smiled. "Thanks for dinner," he muttered
nstead, and dropped a kiss on her nose. He almost
sprinted to the door and his motorcycle. He had to
get away from her long enough to clear his mind. He
started the bike and drove off as though he were
oeing chased by demons. Perhaps he was, he thought.
Somehow, he had to exorcise these emotions that

caused him to say or do things that he might regret later. The cool air on his face would revive him. He hoped.

Ashley slathered the bluish-gray paint across the boards with a brush and watched the porous wood suck it up like a giant sponge. This would never do, she told herself. She had bought ten gallons of paint but it was going to take twice that much. She glanced at Chip, perched high on a ladder with his own paintbrush and roller. They had been painting steadily since breakfast. The work was slow and messy, and Ashley, her old shorts and blouse splattered with paint, was beginning to wish they'd never started.

Chip climbed down from the ladder and perused their work. "I would have thought we'd have more painted by now," he said, "but this wood absorbs the paint like crazy."

She nodded. "How many weekends do you think it'll take to finish it?"

Chip started to answer, but the sound of an approaching motorcycle caught his attention. He craned his neck. "It's him, isn't it?"

Ashley glanced around just as Jack pulled into the driveway on his bike, shut off the engine, and climbed off. He reached for the large white package he'd strapped to the back, and made his way across the front yard to the side of the house where Ashley and Chip stood.

"How's it going?" he asked, taking in the freshly painted wood. "Looks great." He wondered if they knew it was going to take several coats of paint on that particular wood to even out the color. He nodded at Chip when the boy met his gaze.

"What are you doing here?" Ashley asked bluntly.

Jack held up the white package. "I brought dinner —country ribs, to be precise."

"But I told you last night—"

"I know what you told me, but you still have to eat. Am I right? Besides, I'm going to help you paint."

If he had expected her to break into a big smile over his announcement, he was going to be sorely disappointed.

"We don't need your help," Chip said matter-of-factly. "Everything is under control."

Ashley had never heard Chip use that tone of voice, and she was surprised. "Chip is right, we're doing just fine."

"Then think how much better you'd do with three people." He held out the wrapped meat. "How about putting this in your refrigerator? I'll use your paintbrush till you can find me a roller and a long handle." Without another word Jack plucked the brush out of her hand and dipped it into the paint bucket. He began painting, his strokes neat and practiced, while Chip and Ashley looked on in amazement.

Jack refused to take a break, even when Ashley carried out a tray of sandwiches and iced tea. He finished the sandwich in three large bites, and washed it down with the tea. From the corner of her eye she saw Chip staring at the man. There was a lot to be said for his painting. Not only was he neat, but he was also fast. They were already half-finished with the back of the house. At the rate they were going, it would take only one or two weekends to finish the house.

"Where'd you learn to paint?" Ashley asked.

"I started working for a painter when I was fourteen years old. I stayed with it till I decided to become a cop. I should have stuck with painting though. It pays more, and there're a lot fewer headaches."

Ashley noticed that although Chip didn't ask Jack any questions, he listened carefully to what the man said. "What made you decide to be a policeman?" she asked.

Jack stopped working and looked at her long and hard. "Am I going to have to paint your house and answer all your questions as well?"

Ashley smiled. "I can't help it."

Chip laughed out loud. "You're not the only one she questions like that," he said. "She does it to everybody. You should hear what I go through every time I come in from a date." As if suddenly realizing he had the attention of both adults, Chip blushed and put on his serious expression once more.

"Well?" Ashley insisted. "Are you going to tell me or not?" She leaned over and dipped her paintbrush into the can of paint. She was responsible for painting the trim, and for the life of her she couldn't understand why Jack would choose the messiest painter for that job. She was going to have a heck of a time cleaning the windows when the painting was done.

Jack was pondering her question. "One of my brothers almost died at fifteen from a drug overdose. He's clean now, but I decided then and there I wanted to do something about drugs. I figured the police department was the best place to start."

"So did you accomplish what you'd set out to do?"

Jack shrugged. "What can one man do?" He dipped his roller into the metal paint tray. "So what made you decide to be a librarian?"

Ashley chuckled at the question, but she couldn't help but wonder if Jack was truly interested or merely trying to be polite. Then it occurred to her that Jack Sloan wasn't one to do anything unless he wanted to.

"Guess I got lucky, huh?" she said, then paused. "Actually, I had wanted to teach school, but there were no openings for teachers. I took a job as a librarian in an elementary school instead, and I've been doing that kind of work ever since. I used what talents I had as a teacher on Chip." She heard her son laugh from atop the ladder. "He'll tell you what a natural-born teacher I am. He knew his ABCs, could add and subtract before he started school. She beamed proudly at her son. "He's always been at the top of his class."

Chip gave her a derisive smile. "It's not easy having to live with that, Mother," he said. "Most kids don't care to associate with the class brain, as they call me."

"And who's going to care what the other kids think when you're a great scientist searching for a cure for cancer or AIDs?" She didn't wait for him to answer. "You're my superstar, Chip. You're going to do big things with your life."

Jack glanced up at Chip in time to see the smile fade from his lips. In his opinion Ashley had just draped one hell of an expectation over the boy's thin shoulders. As if proving that point, Chip suddenly slumped against the ladder.

"I never made the honor roll in school," Jack said.

"I was too interested in sports and girls and fast cars. I just did what I had to do to get by." He looked at Chip. "You must stay pretty busy during the school year, keeping up with your grades and working too."

"He can do it," Ashley said confidently. "Chip has never let me down."

"Well, I hope he does a better job in school than you're doing on that trim," Jack pointed out.

She stopped painting and examined her work. "What's wrong with it?"

"If you ever have to make a living painting houses, you're going to be out of luck."

The sun was low in the sky when they put their paintbrushes away for the day. "I can't believe we got so much done," Ashley said, as they walked toward the house to clean up. Chip lagged behind. "We owe it all to you."

"Your son didn't do such a bad job himself," Jack said. Chip shot him an appreciative look.

Once Jack had cleaned up at the kitchen sink, he pulled the barbecue grill from the garage and slipped off the protective cover. It looked almost new. Obviously, Ashley didn't do much cooking out. Well, he'd have to change all that. It wasn't until after he'd prepared the ribs that he pondered his previous thoughts. Was he planning on hanging around long enough to make changes in her? he wondered.

In one afternoon he'd learned more about her than in all the hours they'd spent together working. He knew she was a devoted mother, and had probably been a devoted wife as well. She wanted a lot for her children; that was obvious in her conversation with

Chip. He wondered if Chip's own plans for his life were as ambitious as those she'd mentioned. And what about Mikie?

Jack was surprised by his own line of thought. Here he was playing private detective in Ashley's life when he should have been figuring out what to do with his own. There was something strange about a man who preferred living in a boardinghouse to having a home of his own. He hadn't really thought about it until Ashley had brought it to his attention. He'd rented the place after his marriage and job had fallen apart, although he still couldn't figure out which one had crumbled first. In the beginning he'd told people he and his wife had split up because she couldn't handle being married to a cop, worrying about him getting shot and all. But that wasn't it. He'd left her because she'd slept with half the police force before they were married, and hadn't broken off all her relationships after the wedding as she'd said she would. He couldn't endure the snickering that had gone on behind his back.

He hated the memory of how weak he'd been then. Why hadn't he walked out in the beginning, while he still had his self-respect? Perhaps it was because he had a hell of a caseload at work. Or maybe it was because she'd been raised by parents like his, and he felt sorry for her. It took two bullet holes and a couple of weeks in a hospital bed, during which time he'd done a lot of thinking, before he'd convinced himself to leave.

Jack searched the garage until he found a bag of charcoal and a can of lighter fluid. He dumped charcoal into the grill and squirted on the little bit of lighter fluid that was left. He didn't like to think about his ex-wife. He believed in moving forward in life, not drowning in memories of the past. Still, he had changed as a result of his past.

Jack's musings were interrupted when Ashley pulled the sliding door open and carried out the plate of ribs. "Did you find everything you need?" she asked. When he nodded, she set the plate of ribs on the picnic table and sat down. "I feel much better after my shower," she said. "You're welcome to take one."

Jack gazed at her. She looked so fresh and clean, he could almost smell the soap from where he was standing. "I'd be wasting my time," he said. "I didn't think to bring a change of clothes." Jack suddenly realized by the uncomfortable look on her face that he was staring. He looked away, but in his mind he could still see her. At one time he'd thought he would never be attracted to another woman emotionally. He hadn't let anyone come close in so long.

"You sure are deep in thought today," Ashley said, noting his silence. A scowl deepened the wedge between his thick brows.

Jack shrugged. "I've got a lot on my mind."

"Anything you care to talk about?"

Jack's gaze met hers briefly, and he knew that if there was anyone in the world he'd want to share his thoughts with, it would be Ashley. She inspired confidence, but at the moment he wasn't in the mood to talk about himself. He wanted to know more about her. "Why'd you get divorced?" he blurted out before he could stop himself.

Ashley was surprised by the abrupt question, and it showed in her face. "My husband found someone else," she said softly.

He waited for her to add something more, but she didn't. "End of story?" he asked.

She shrugged and gave him the briefest of smiles. "I don't know what more I can tell you."

"Whose fault was it?"

"Whose fault? I don't think you can put all the blame on one person. I blamed my ex-husband for leaving me for someone else, but I probably disappointed him as well. He said he couldn't talk to me, and that I pushed him constantly. That I couldn't accept him the way he was, and I expected more of him than he could give."

"Did you?"

She pondered the question. "Now that I look back, I see where I went wrong. But he went wrong too, when he decided to have nothing to do with his children after the divorce."

Jack nodded as he picked up the ribs with the pair of tongs she'd provided. He noticed Ashley was watching him thoughtfully. "Why are you looking at me like that?"

"Like what?"

"Like you're trying to burn a hole through my forehead with your eyes so you can find out what I'm thinking."

"Am I that obvious?"

He nodded. "You don't exactly have a poker face. Now what d'you want to know?"

"Well, now that I've told you what went wrong in my marriage, I want you to tell me about yours."

Jack rolled his eyes and muttered a curse. He set the empty plate on the picnic table and crossed his arms over his wide chest. "You are one hell of a curious woman, you know that? Okay, ask me anything."

"Why did the two of you split up?"

"Easy question. We were unfaithful to each other," he said, not wanting her to know it had been his wife who'd been unfaithful to him.

Ashley didn't blink an eye over the confession. "Where'd you meet?"

"In the bar where she danced. Me and my buddies from the force went there when we were off duty."

Ashley nodded. She would think about it later, she told herself, but right now she wanted information, and Jack seemed willing to give it. "What was she like?"

Jack thought about it. "She was a looker, but she had a hard time with serious relationships. I thought I could change all that, but I didn't. Instead, our problems got in the way of my work." He paused. "I couldn't seem to get my head on straight. When I was at work, all I could think about was her, wondering where she was and what she was doing. I already knew I couldn't trust her. Then, when I was with her, I couldn't take my mind off the cases I was working on. When the day of the bust came, I had a bad feeling, but I didn't know if it was the case or my marriage messing up my head. I had this feeling in my gut that something bad was going down. And it did."

Ashley gazed at the pained expression on his face. "That's when your buddies were shot?"

He nodded. "Both sides got hit pretty bad. I left the force soon afterward, about the same time I ditched my marriage." His smile eased the sudden tension between them. "Now, you know all about me, more than anybody else knows, in fact." He paused. "Aren't you going to say anything? Since I met you, I've never known you to be this silent."

"I'm sorry you had to go through all that."

"Squash the pity routine, Sherlock."

She arched one brow. "I don't feel sorry for you, Jack. I'm happy for you."

"Come again?"

"I think it's wonderful that you rose above all that adversity. I'm sure it made you a stronger person."

Jack pondered her words. How did she always manage to say the right thing? he wondered. And how come he'd just emptied his guts at her feet? Now, she knew everything. Wasn't it just like a woman to try to get all the information she could from a man?

And wasn't it like a woman to make you fall in love with her, just when you thought you could make it without her?

Nine

They finished painting the house two weeks later, after having worked a total of three weekends. Jack insisted they celebrate, but Chip bowed out, saying he had previous plans. Jack didn't know whether to believe the boy or not. Although Chip was civil to him, Jack still sensed an underlying hostility. Mikie was no problem; in fact, he seemed to look forward to Jack's visits. And Ashley always looked happy to see him in the evenings.

Jack had reconciled himself to the fact that he was in love with Ashley. He no longer plotted ways to get rid of her; on the contrary, they spent most of their waking hours together.

"So where do the two of you want to go for dinner?" Jack asked, having showered and changed clothes. Ashley had showered as well, and was dressed in a blue jumpsuit and coordinating scarf.

"I want pizza!" Mikie declared, jumping up and down in the backseat of Jack's car.

"Pizza is fine with me," Ashley said, noting how handsome, not to mention sexy, Jack looked in a pair of new jeans. His hair was still wet from his shower, and curled well past the collar of an aquamarine shirt.

Ashley and Mikie played a word game as Jack drove to the pizza parlor. He couldn't help but envy the close, easygoing relationship between Ashley and her son. It was the same with Chip. He wondered for a moment what it would be like to have a child, someone who would look up to him, someone who would make him a silly card for Father's Day. Or someone who would be happy just to see him at the end of the day.

Of course, being a father entailed a lot of hard work and responsibility. It didn't look like an easy task at all. He had watched Ashley in her parental role for the past two weeks. But she didn't seem to mind the demands motherhood made on her. She gave freely of her time and love. As childish as it seemed, at first he had almost resented it, until he realized there was more than enough to go around.

The pizza parlor was crowded with high school kids. "You find a table and I'll place the order," Jack said to Ashley, trying to make himself heard over the noise. After having shared several pizzas with them over the past couple of weeks, he knew what they liked. While Jack and Ashley waited for their order, Mikie, clutching a fistful of quarters, scrambled to the back of the room where the pinball machines stood.

"I wish you wouldn't spoil him like that," Ashley said. "I can't afford to hand out money like you do, and I don't want him to get used to it. Who knows—" She bit back the rest of her words and looked away.

Jack noticed the faint color on her cheeks. "What were you going to say?"

"Forget it."

"You were going to say something like who knows how long I'll be around. Right?"

Her face reddened. "Something like that."

Jack studied her. She had every right to feel the way she did. He never made dates with her in advance; instead, he'd phone her at the last minute to make plans. More often than not, she would refuse, telling him she couldn't get a baby-sitter for Mikie. He sometimes wondered if she was doing it on purpose, trying to teach him a lesson perhaps. He would then suggest cooking out on her barbecue grill. Not much of a date, he thought.

The thing that struck him the funniest was his desire to be with her all the time. He liked her cozy home with its warm earth tones, wicker baskets, dried flowers, and comfortable furniture in pretty prints. And it always smelled as though she'd just taken an apple pie out of the oven. His place smelled like dirty laundry, and before he'd quit smoking, stale cigarettes. It didn't matter that he was with her all day. As soon as he dropped her off at the office, he began missing her all over again.

The nights were the worst. He lay in bed sometimes for hours thinking about her, how good she'd feel next to him, beneath him. He tried not to think of the night they'd spent in each other's arms. Ashley had called it a mistake, while he thought it the most wonderful thing that had ever happened to him. Because of her feelings, he hadn't invited her back, but that didn't mean it wasn't on his mind much of the time. In fact, he'd done his share of pacing the floor because of it. It was nights such as those that he searched his soul for his feelings about her, turning over the questions and answers, trying to examine each one. Sometimes he got the impression that she was as eager as he to share his bed again, but he couldn't work up the nerve to ask her, and that made him feel like an adolescent.

"They're calling our number," Ashley said for the second time, wondering what had put such an odd look on Jack's face. He was certainly deep in thought tonight.

Jack blinked. He glanced blankly at the ticket in his hand. He'd been daydreaming again, something he had become quite good at lately. He glanced at Ashley and found her watching him curiously, and wondered if everybody who was in love acted the way he did. That's because the day-to-day things didn't matter to him anymore. All he could think about was Ashley. He didn't want to think about showering or eating or working or the other countless and meaningless things that cluttered his life.

Jack paid for the pizza and carried it back to the table. Mikie had returned, having spent all his money on the games. Jack set the pizza in the center of the table, and Ashley picked up the hot slices one by one and placed them on paper plates. Jack loved to watch her slender, graceful hands, and his stomach knotted as he remembered those same hands on his body. They could catch a teardrop on a child's cheek or stroke a lover tenderly. Damn, he was doing it again.

"How is it?" Jack asked Mikie once the pizza was

cool enough to eat. Perhaps he could steer his thoughts in a different direction.

The boy chewed and swallowed. "This is the best one yet," he announced.

Jack grinned. He was a cute kid. He looked like his mother. "You say that every time," Jack reminded him.

Once they arrived home, Mikie suggested they watch a video movie. Jack made himself comfortable on the couch, knowing he was in for a long evening. But he would have sat through the entire Civil War if it meant spending time with Ashley.

Some time later, Jack opened his eyes, just as the credits flashed across the television screen. He had fallen asleep on the sofa while watching *Lady and the Tramp*. He blinked several times. Mikie had fallen asleep as well, sprawled on the floor in front of the television set. Jack looked over at Ashley, who was stretched out on the love seat. She smiled at him.

"Welcome back. And don't ever try to convince me you don't snore."

Jack sat up and rubbed his eyes with the balls of his fists. "How long did I sleep?"

"You fell asleep right after Jim Dear and Darling's baby was born."

"Jim Dear and Darling? Who—"

"They're the couple who owned Lady. You really did miss a lot." She glanced at her sleeping son. "Looks like I'm the only one who made it through the entire movie."

Jack stood. "Want me to carry him to bed?"

"I would appreciate it. He's too heavy for me."

Jack scooped the boy easily from the floor and followed Ashley up the stairs to his room, which was decorated in bright, cheerful colors. Along one wall stood a bookcase crammed full of picture books and a children's encyclopedia. A small desk sat off to one side, its top bearing a page from a coloring book that hadn't yet been finished.

It was a room a child would feel comfortable and secure in, Jack thought, as he placed the boy gently on his bed. Mikie's little arms tightened around Jack's neck briefly, long enough to have a strong effect on Jack. Ashley began taking off the boy's sneakers and socks while Jack looked on. For a minute he despised the man who'd fathered Mikie and Chip. Not only did he hate him for the years he'd had with Ashley, he hated the man for running out on his family just as his own father had done. It was a hate so powerful, so consuming, it frightened Jack. Yet he was no better, he told himself. He would suffocate under the responsibility of a family. He only had to look at how he'd screwed up his own life.

Jack forced his thoughts aside as Ashley covered Mikie with a bright blue bedspread. He surveyed the room once more, remembering that his own bedroom had looked nothing like the one he was looking at now. The walls in the bedroom he'd shared with four brothers had been a dingy gray color, the sheets threadbare from years of laundering.

Ashley saw the look in Jack's eyes and wished there was something she could do to make it go away. She knew he seldom thought of his past, but when he did, that cold, vacant look would crop up. She wondered if he would ever expose his feelings to another person. Would he ever love and trust another woman enough to share his hurts and joys? Ashley knew then that she would like to be that woman. Instead of saying anything, though, she stood on tiptoe and kissed Jack gently on the lips. Surprise registered on his face and wiped away the look of desolation. Their gazes locked, and something passed between them, something real and powerful, so powerful that she couldn't breathe or think straight for a minute. Ashley clasped his hand in hers and tugged it. He followed her out of the room and down the stairs.

Jack had not missed the almost tangible emotion that had swept over them. He'd felt it as surely as he felt his heart beating in his chest. It was as undeniable as his need to breathe. This was love in its rawest form, he thought.

"Would you like a cup of coffee?" Ashley asked once they'd descended the stairs and reached the kitchen.

Jack nodded. One thing he'd learned to drink a lot of over the past two weeks was coffee. Ashley practically inhaled it. Thankfully, it was decaffeinated.

"What time are you expecting Chip home?" he asked.

"His curfew is midnight," she said, measuring the coffee carefully. "Naturally, most of the kids he hangs around with have later curfews. So we have an unspoken agreement that if he's twenty or thirty minutes late, I don't hassle him. I call it my grace period."

Once the coffee was ready, they took their steaming cups into the living room. Jack waited for Ashley to sit down, then joined her on the couch and set his cup on the coffee table.

Jack draped his arm over Ashley's shoulders and pulled her close for a brief kiss. "You and I haven't had much time alone lately," he said. "Either Jeeter or your kids and their friends or your neighbors are always around."

Ashley smiled. "You sound jealous."

"I am jealous," he said, pulling her tightly against him. "I want you to myself." His hands slid down to the small of her back and massaged it.

Ashley could see the smoky desire in his eyes that made them the color of onyx in the dim light, and she knew he longed for her as much as she did him. But he had backed off the past couple of weeks, and she didn't know what to make of it. In other ways, though, they had grown closer. She had confided in him several times, telling him things she wouldn't have dreamed of telling other people. She had told him of the despair and low self-esteem she'd suffered when her ex-husband had walked out. Her family and friends had never guessed; she'd put up a good front.

At first, Ashley had promised herself not to learn to count on Jack for anything. Even little things, she'd told herself. Even when it seemed he'd made a habit of going by the grocery store after work each day to pick up something to barbecue at her place. Then she caught herself rushing home after work one day to shower and change before he called to make plans, and she stopped herself. If Jack was going to wait until the last minute to invite her out or make plans to have dinner there, he would have to pay the consequences. Sometimes it meant they couldn't go out because she wasn't able to find a sitter, other times it meant he had to cool his heels on the sofa till she showered.

If Jack was confused as to the direction they were traveling, he never indicated it. And while he seemed content to involve her children in their plans, she could sense he wanted more. She often found him watching her from across the dinner table or over a heated game of Monopoly. She could clearly read the need in his eyes. But Jack wasn't the only one watching. Chip watched her constantly.

Jack slid his free arm around Ashley's waist as he nibbled an earlobe. She seemed to have a lot on her mind tonight, but that didn't keep her from shivering when his warm breath fanned her ear. He inhaled her perfume with every raspy breath he took. He would recognize the scent of her anywhere. It was as ingrained in his mind as her face was. His mouth inched down her slender neck and came to a rest at her pulse point. It hammered frantically against his lips.

Dazed, Ashley felt as though her body were melting into the sofa. Jack covered her breasts with his palms, and the warmth of his hands seeped through the material of her jumpsuit. She closed her eyes, branding the memory of the way her nipples felt as he gently rubbed them between his thumb and forefinger into her mind. Ashley realized they had gone too far—she could feel it low in her belly. Her body was sensitized to his every touch. When he kissed her, she met the thrust of his tongue boldly. She nibbled his ear and took delight when he shivered as she had. When Jack lifted her high in his arms and carried her into her bedroom, Ashley was too far gone to offer an argument. Her body was on fire, and Jack Sloan was the man she wanted to quench it.

Jack could think of a million reasons not to make love to the woman in his arms. First of all, this was the house where her children lived. Yes, but Chip wasn't expected home for a while. There was still plenty of time.

Ashley tightened her arms around his neck and pulled him close. Her mouth was hot against his. Jack felt himself weakening. Ah, damn. Her lips were damp and swollen, her breasts soft, and she arched against him in a way that made him crazy. He ached for her with every fiber of his body, every breath he took, every beat of his heart. It was dangerous to want a woman that badly, he thought, as he placed her gently on the bed. There was no stopping him now.

It was like watching a movie in slow motion, Ashley thought, as Jack made love to her. He kissed her hands, then ran his tongue along each tapered finger. When he'd kissed that area thoroughly, he moved to her wrist. He smiled when he found her pulse beating a frantic message to the rest of her body. His lips crept up her arm to the inside of her elbow, making the downy hairs on her flesh stand up straight. Chills zigzagged along her spine and spread like wildfire to the network of nerve endings and pleasure points throughout her being.

Once Jack had removed all of her clothes, he gazed at her lovingly. It jolted him when he realized just how much he cared for the lovely creature before him. It was scary to love or want *anything* that much. Scarier still was the fact he wanted only her and for all time. He was tempted to sit back on his heels and think that one through. The mere thought resonated with responsibility and obligation.

Jack pressed his face against Ashley's breasts before skimming his lips along the valley between and down her flat stomach to her navel. He reacquainted himself with the satiny smoothness of her thighs. When he had nipped and kissed her inner thighs thoroughly, he buried his face against the ebony curls where her thighs joined and dipped his tongue inside. The crisp curls tickled his lips, and the musky scent of her body almost sent him over the edge. She moaned and arched against him, and plunged her fingers through his hair.

Jack waited until after he was certain Ashley had climaxed before peeling off his own clothes. The look on her face told him she was pleased with what she saw, and she greeted him with a honeyed warmth that fit around him like a tight sheath. Every time he thrust into her, he had to grit his teeth and fight for self-control. Only when Ashley pinnacled once again did he allow himself that freedom. Together they spiraled and floated back to earth, each chanting the other's name.

Jack saw to it that they were both up and dressed immediately afterward. He'd been tempted to lie in bed and hold Ashley in his arms. In fact, he'd been tempted to tell her how much he loved her, but the time wasn't right. For one thing they had no idea at what moment her older son would walk through the door, or if Mikie would wake up and want a glass of water. Knowing Ashley as he did, Jack realized that any embarrassing confrontation with her sons would leave her mortified and guilt-stricken for the rest of her life.

As if reading his thoughts, Ashley glanced up from her place at the kitchen table. "We should never have . . . well, you know . . . taken such a chance. I don't know what came over me."

"Don't say it," he interrupted, pressing an index finger to her lips. "We didn't plan it, it just happened. And it was wonderful." It was inconceivable to him that she could feel so guilty over something so wonderful. For him it was like a rebirth.

After the last time they'd made love, it had improved his disposition tenfold. Jack had found himself whistling in the mornings, something he hadn't done in years. Food had tasted better. He'd caught his reflection one day as he paused just outside the bank and had frowned at the haphazardly dressed man before him. Lord, his jeans were threadbare and faded and hadn't seen an ironing in years. His T-shirt was too tight after having been laundered more times than he could count. What did Ashley see in him? he'd wondered. He'd gone shopping for clothes that same day.

"That's easy for you to say," Ashley spouted. "You've never had children." She was piqued that he hadn't revealed his feelings to her during their lovemaking. She had wanted to confess her love for him, but had bitten back the words before they left her lips. She would not make a fool of herself in front of Jack Sloan. Surely to heaven he cared for her just a little, she told herself. Or did he? She was beginning to wonder exactly what she *did* mean to him, especially now that she had taken such a risk by allowing him in her bedroom. Any other man would have been tossed out by the seat of his pants.

Jack could sense that her thoughts were churning inside her head just by the look on her face.

Instead of confronting her, he leaned over and kissed her on the cheek. Her body was stiff and unyielding.

"Why don't I make you a cup of coffee?" he suggested. When she merely shrugged, he got up and started the coffee. He paced the floor waiting for it to drip through.

Ashley couldn't bear the silence, or the gurgling sound of the coffee maker. She climbed the stairs to Mikie's room and peeked in. He was sleeping soundly, a stuffed dog tucked in one arm. She entered the kitchen a moment later and found Jack pouring her coffee.

Jack placed the fresh cup of coffee on the kitchen table in front of her. She responded with a word of thanks. "It's late," she said. "You should go."

"I want to wait with you till Chip comes home."

"You don't have to. I'm fine. Really." Her tone was flat, void of emotion, but the look in her eyes told him she wanted to be alone. Jack hesitated before dropping a kiss on her forehead. Finally, he made his way to the front door. "Call me if he doesn't get here soon," he said over his shoulder, but there was no answer. He let himself out the front door and crossed the lawn to where his car sat on the side of the road. He hated to leave her, but worse yet was sitting there under her gaze with so many questions unanswered and so many decisions to make.

He loved her and he wanted her, just as much as he wanted his next breath. Yet he couldn't imagine marrying a woman with kids, one of them almost grown. If that wasn't bad enough, there would be the mortgage payment, the doctor bills . . . and hadn't Ashley mentioned something about Mikie needing braces? Money wasn't really an issue—he had saved plenty. But men who took on entire families should be much more stable than he was, more responsible.

He was still a coward at heart.

Ashley sat on the sofa and pretended to be interested in the movie on television. Time crept by, which meant she had plenty of it on her hands to wonder where her son was and to think about Jack. When the hands on the clock pointed to 12:45 A.M. she didn't blink an eye. At one o'clock she crossed her arms and pressed her lips into a grim line.

Chip had better have a good explanation.

Jack pulled into the parking lot of the boarding-house and muttered a four-letter word when he found a car sitting in his parking space. He blinked, realizing suddenly it was Ashley's car. He parked beside it, climbed out of his car, and hurried around to the other one. When he reached it, he found Chip slumped in the front seat.

At first there was fear, white-hot terror that something awful had happened to Ashley's son, and that she would have to endure heartache. The emotion was so real that it left a bad taste in his mouth. He would prefer ripping his own heart out of his chest. He almost tore the door off its hinges trying to get to the boy. But after further examination he saw Chip was drunk.

Jack hoisted the boy over one shoulder and carried him from the car to his room. He dumped him on the bed unceremoniously, made a pot of coffee, then scrambled some eggs. Once finished with that chore, he dragged Chip into the shower and turned on the cold water full force. Chip squealed like a baby pig, and woke up sputtering.

"Why the hell did you do that!" he demanded. Water sluiced down his face into his eyes. His clothes were saturated.

"You came to my door, kiddo," Jack said, sarcasm lacing his tone. "I can only *imagine* what your mother would have done under the same circumstances."

Chip frowned. "She treats me like a baby," he bellowed angrily.

Jack suddenly reached for him, grabbing him up by the collar of his shirt. "Let me tell you something, punk." His look was menacing. "The next time I find you driving under the influence, I'm going to kick your butt from here to kingdom come. You got that?"

Chip swallowed, and his Adam's apple bobbed in his throat. "I got it," he muttered.

Jack let him go with such force he almost fell. "Next time you want to party with your buddies, you call me to come get you. Now get those wet things off and wrap up in that bathrobe." He pointed to the robe hanging on the back of the door. "Your breakfast is waiting."

"I'm not hungry."

"You'll eat if I have to shovel it down your throat."

When Chip exited the bathroom wearing Jack's robe, his look was sullen. Jack motioned for him to sit at the table, and the boy did as he was told. "I don't like eggs."

"You do now."

"Why are you treating me like a kid? I shouldn't have come here in the first place. I should have gone home."

"Yeah, so your mother could have seen you in that

condition. Great idea." He pointed to the plate of food. "Eat."

Chip ate his toast and forced the scrambled eggs down. When he was finished, he placed his knife and fork on the plate and pushed it away. He stared at Jack for a full minute before he said anything. "Why are you looking at me like that?"

Jack wished he had a cigarette. He wasn't used to kids, especially troubled teenagers. He didn't quite know what to do, and the enormity of what could have happened frightened him. But he'd be damned if he'd let Chip see it.

Jack leaned back in his chair and propped his feet on another. "What happened tonight?"

Chip didn't answer right away, and for a moment it looked as though he had no intention of doing so. Jack waited, his eyes trained on Chip's, knowing he'd wait the kid out forever if he had to. Chip was smart, Jack told himself. Smart enough to figure out if the older man was calling his bluff. One slip and he would lose the kid's respect once and for all.

Chip refused to meet Jack's steady gaze. "You'll think it's stupid."

"Try me."

"My girlfriend broke up with me tonight."

"Why?"

"She says I don't spend enough time with her. Says she's tired of sitting home while her friends get to have all the fun."

"And do you spend enough time with her?"

"No," Chip said. "We barely dated during the school year. Between work and studies and keeping an eye on Mikie—" He shrugged. "It doesn't matter now."

"What did you do after she broke up with you?"

"I took her home, then stopped by a convience store. I asked this guy to buy me a six-pack of beer. Don't ask me why, I know it was stupid. Then I drove around for a while until I came upon this park. I sat on a picnic table . . . just thinking . . . and drinking beer. I guess I lost track of time."

"Yeah, I guess you did."

Chip studied the man across the table. "What now?"

Jack unfolded himself from the chair and stretched. "You need to go to bed. You can sleep here. I'll carry your wet clothes to the dryer."

Chip hesitated. "What about . . . my mother?"

"I'll handle that. This time," he added. "In the meantime you figure out how you can learn how to handle disappointment without getting sloppy drunk."

Chip blushed profusely. "Uh, Jack?"

"Yeah?"

"That was the first and only time I've ever . . . ever done anything like that . . . get drunk, I mean. I swear."

"I don't care if it was your first or not," Jack replied matter-of-factly. "I just hope it's your last."

Chip was snoring gently by the time Jack let himself out the door. He drove straight to Ashley's, and wasn't surprised to find a patrol car parked on the side of the road. The front door was thrown open the minute he knocked.

"Oh, it's you," Ashley said dully, her eyes bright with tears.

"Chip's okay," he said, and watched her go limp

ith relief. He assured the policeman that the boy as okay, and the officer left.

Ashley was full of questions. "Where is he now? 'hat happened?"

Jack told her about Chip's girlfriend breaking up ith him, leaving out the part about the boy getting runk. He figured it was up to Chip to tell her—if he anted her to know. "So I fixed him a bite to eat and ent him to bed. He's sleeping on my couch."

Ashley could feel the anger building up inside. 'ou mean he has been back all this time, and you idn't so much as pick up the telephone!" She almost shrieked the accusation. *Do you realize I 'as half out of my mind with worry?* And why idn't you send him home?"

Jack sighed and shook his head from side to side. thought I was doing the right thing, okay? I mean, le kid was just late coming home, for Pete's sake. e didn't rob a bank." Jack put both hands on her noulders. "Look, you know how kids are at that ge. They're not as responsible as adults. Chip just st track of time."

Ashley stared at him as though he'd just grown orns. "You of all people shouldn't criticize others bout responsibility, Jack Sloan," she said hotly. "I an't count on you to make it to dinner on time. In ict, I can't count on your for anything, not even to ring my son home."

When Jack spoke, his voice was controlled. "I wasn't riticizing the boy, Ashley. I was trying to stand up r him. You're so hard on the kid, you forget he's nly sixteen years old. If you don't stop pushing, ou're going to push him right out the front door."

"Just what makes you such an expert on human-

kind, Jack? You gave up on people a long time ago
She was hurting, and she wanted to hurt him bac'
Why hadn't Chip come to *her* with his problems?

"You're happy to be with someone who doesr
step over that imaginary line you've drawn arour
you. You want the good things in life—love, peop
who care about you—but you don't want the oblig
tions. And yet you have the audacity to come in'
my house and tell me how to raise my children." SI
had to pause to catch her breath. "I think you shou'
leave. And stay away," she added.

Jack's face was like granite. "Gladly," he said. F
stalked toward the door and let himself out. F
wanted to hit something, anything. Once inside h
car, he slammed the door with all his might. The ca
rocked on its wheels. It wasn't until he was on tl
main road that he relaxed his grip on the steerir
wheel.

He'd been a fool to try to help Ashley. For one bri
moment, he'd wanted to share her troubles. That
what love was all about, wasn't it? He had convince
himself she needed him, that taking responsibili
was just another way of showing love. When yo
loved somebody, the obligations didn't seem so ove
whelming. And she had kicked him in the teetl
But wasn't that the way it always turned out whe
you tried to do something for somebody?

Ashley couldn't sleep. She reached for the lamp o
her nightstand and turned it on. She had read ever
magazine she owned. She propped up her pillow
and leaned back, staring straight ahead at nothin
in particular. She focused on the collage of picture
over her bureau that depicted Chip and Mikie's li
up till now. Chip at birth, and again at two. Mikie :

irth. Chip in kindergarten, and another picture
aken in first grade. How had Chip got all the way
rom first grade to high school in such a short time?
he wondered.

Ashley's heart felt heavy. Jack was right. She did
xpect too much from Chip, and she would probably
xpect just as much from Mikie in the future. She'd
lone it to keep them from being tiny replicas of
heir father. She'd wanted to raise her children to be
nature and responsible. She wanted her sons to be
good citizens, men that people could look up to. She
vas going to have to loosen up or lose them.

Her brow wrinkled in thought. Jack was all those
hings, and look what a free spirit he was. And
when it came down to it, he was as responsible and
caring as the next person. She respected him. Per-
naps that was what counted most.

Heaven help her, she loved him with all her heart.
And she had thrown him out of her house.

Ten

When Ashley opened her eyes the following morn ing, Chip was standing in the doorway to her bed room. "May I come in?" he asked, not quite meeting her gaze.

Ashley sat up and propped a pillow behind her "Please do." She watched Chip cross the room, and as he attempted to sit at the foot of the bed, she stopped him. "Sit here next to me," she said, pat ting the spot beside her.

Chip moved closer. He didn't speak right away but when he did, his voice cracked with emotion "I'm sorry," he said. "I know I let you down. Just like Dad let you down so many times."

"Oh, Chip—" Ashley saw the despair on his face and thought her heart would break. She reached for her son, and he buried his face against her neck "You could never let me down. You have always been there for me—you're the bright spot in my life. When your father left, and I didn't think I could go on, you

couraged me. You have been my friend as well as
y son." Once she opened up to him, the words just
illed from her mouth. "I'm the one who should
ologize," she said gently. When Chip looked up in
urprise, she continued, "I've always expected too
uch from you. I wanted you to be my son, my
iend, my confidant, Mikie's surrogate father and
le model—and to bring home the best grades in
hool while you worked as well. I thought it would
ake you more mature, responsible. I never thought
the burden—" She had to stop talking to catch
er breath.

Chip looked as though he might cry. He rubbed
s eyes. "I knew you wanted me to grow up differ-
it from Dad," he said solemnly.

She nodded. "And that's not fair to you. You need
be your own person. I'm proud of the young man
u've become, Chip, but I want you to have this
me to just concentrate on being sixteen years
d." She paused. "I'd like for you to quit your job. I
ant you to be able to do the things your friends do.
think, after a while, you and Jill will patch things
p."

Chip stared at his hands and shook his head as
ough trying to figure out why his mother had had
change of heart. "Did Jack call you?" he asked,
oking up at her.

"He dropped by last night to let me know you were
kay. Why?"

He shrugged. "Just wondering, that's all. He's an
kay guy, I guess." He grinned. "That is, if you like
vergrown hippies."

Ashley blushed like a schoolgirl. "I do," she con-
ssed. "I really do."

*   *   *

Two hours later, Ashley walked into the agen[cy]
and found Jeeter talking with another man. S[he]
nodded to both, took a seat at Jack's desk, an[d]
prepared to wait for him.

Jeeter glanced up at his niece. Although he did[n't]
say anything, he would have to have been blind [to]
overlook the tired, distraught expression on her fac[e.]
"Jack's not coming in today," he said.

"Oh?" Ashley tried to conceal her disappointmen[t,]
but it was not easy hiding things from a man who['d]
spent thirty years of his life digging up informatio[n.]

"He took a few days off. As hard as he works, [I]
figured he needed it. You could use the rest to[o.]
Now come over and meet my friend." He motione[d]
her over.

"This is Sergeant Flannery," Jeeter said, noddi[ng]
his head toward a man who looked to be close to h[is]
age. "He's retired now, but he was Jack's superi[or]
when Jack was on the police force. He was in th[e]
neighborhood and stopped by." Jeeter made a *tskin[g]*
sound as he regarded the man. "Jack will be disa[p]-
pointed he missed you."

"I doubt it," he said, his expression somber. "Th[is]
isn't the first time I've dropped by to see him. He['s]
never here, and he doesn't return my phone calls."

Ashley's interest was piqued by this bit of info[r]-
mation. She held her hand out in greeting, and th[e]
man shook it. "Did you know Jack at the time of th[e]
bust?"

Sergeant Flannery looked surprised, but nodde[d]
without asking her to clarify her question. "I did. [He]
reported to me. It was one of the biggest cocain[e]
busts, if not *the* biggest that Atlanta has ever seen[.]

Ashley smiled at him prettily. "I was on my way to the Waffle House when I dropped by, Sergeant. Could I buy you breakfast?"

Jeeter didn't blink an eye at the request, and Ashley wondered if he knew she was trying to get information from the sergeant. Of course he did, she told herself. Jeeter was like a wise old owl—he watched but never interfered.

The sergeant looked as if he might topple over in his chair at Ashley's invitation. "Why, I'd consider it an honor, lass," he said, surprise ringing loud in his voice.

"Uncle Jeeter?"

Jeeter shook his head. "I can't, sugar. I'm expecting an important phone call."

"We'll only be gone a short while," Ashley told him, "then I'll take over the phones for you." The sergeant pulled himself up from the chair and offered Ashley his arm. She smiled and took it.

Once at the restaurant, Ashley found herself enjoying the conversation with Sergeant Flannery, or Patrick, as he'd told her to call him. She nibbled on a piece of toast while he wolfed down a three-egg omelet, sausage, and homemade biscuits with gravy.

" 'Course, when I was a rookie, we didn't have the problem with drugs that we have today," he said between mouthfuls. "Or the violence. Sure, we had our barroom brawls and domestic problems, but nothing like you see on the streets today. It takes a damn good cop to make it in today's world."

"Was Jack a good cop?"

The sergeant arched his thick eyebrows. "So it's

Jack you want to know about, eh? You in love with him?"

Ashley nodded. "He doesn't know."

"I find that hard to believe, lass. That boy knows everything." He paused. "You asked me if he was a good cop. I suppose I'd have to answer yes and no."

Ashley leaned forward. "Why do you say that?"

The sergeant straightened in his seat. "He was a damn good police officer in the line of duty. Never complained, did his job the best he could. He was a hero ten times over. He trained some fine men over the years. But he was soft. He made excuses for his men."

Ashley shook her head. "That doesn't sound like the Jack I know."

" 'Course it doesn't. Life does funny things to us. He's grown hard and tough as leather. He'd make a terrific cop now."

Ashley shook her head. "I think there's a lot to be said for compassion, Sergeant. Even in our police force." The man shrugged. Ashley wasn't about to try to change his mind at his age. Her real concern was Jack.

"Can you tell me about the big bust?"

"What do you want to know?"

"About the two men who go shot."

The man's face clouded over. "Yeah, well, they were rookies. Their first bust, you know. Jack didn't want them in on it, said they weren't ready. Like I told you, he made excuses for his men." The sergeant shoved his plate aside and clasped his hands together on the table. "It was a nasty scene, seemed like half the town got shot up that night. They—the dealers, I mean—had big guns. I'm talking mag-

nums, automatics. Hell, when it was all over, it
ooked like the army had come through. We're not
talking about some small-time drug pushers—these
guys were out-and-out magnates of the drug world."

"Do you think somebody tipped off the dealers?"
she asked.

The sergeant didn't answer right away. "Jack
thought so. He said he didn't feel right about the
bust. He wanted to hold off. But the district attor-
ney was on my back constantly. It was reelection
time, and he wasn't the popular choice. That kind of
bust gets a lot of votes. So Jack went in. He bought
two bullets in the back, trying to save his men. One
got him near his kidney, and the other punctured a
hole in his lung. Thank God they fixed it." He sat
there quietly for a moment, as though deep in
thought. "One other thing. A couple of witnesses
said it looked like Jack *wanted* to get shot up."

Ashley gasped. "You mean he wanted *to die*? But
why?"

"Trouble at home. Not to mention seeing his men
shot up like that. He felt responsible. I heard ru-
mors about his home life, but I don't think it's my
place to be spreading them further. I'm sure Jack
will tell you if he wants you to know. A man's got his
right to privacy, if you know what I mean."

Ashley smiled, but she could feel the tears welling
up in her eyes. "Thank you, Sergeant."

The man pulled himself up from the booth. "Thank
you, lassie. I don't talk about this often, and it feels
good to get it off my chest. I'll rest easier knowing
Jack has somebody like you around to take care of
him."

When Ashley returned to the office, she took over

the telephones for Jeeter and typed several letters and reports. There was a wire basket full of filing. She was determined to stay busy. It kept her mind off Jack. Well, not really, she told herself.

When five o'clock rolled around, Ashley closed up and locked the door. She drove straight to Jack's place and sat in the parking lot, waiting and wishing for him to come home. He never did.

By the time Ashley fell into bed that night, her stomach was tied in knots. She called Jack's number for the umpteenth time, but there was no answer. She didn't sleep much that night, and when she stumbled into the kitchen the following morning, she felt exhausted and bedraggled. Her mood was no better.

"You'll feel better after this cup of coffee," Chip assured her. "I even poured it into your favorite cup, see? The one that says, 'Life begins at Menopause.' Would you like toast?"

"I'm not hungry."

"You didn't eat dinner last night. Did you skip lunch yesterday too?"

"Are you taking a census?"

"Has this glum mood got anything to do with Jack the hippie?"

"Stop talking about him like that." she mumbled. "He may be your new father one day."

Chip's eyes widened. "For real?" He didn't give her a chance to answer. "Are you going to make him stop wearing jeans and start wearing polyester pants and double-knit shirts like my friends' fathers?"

Ashley shook her head. "I like Jack Sloan just the

way he is." She frowned. "And if I ever see him again, I'm going to tell him just that."

Jack pulled into the parking lot of the motorcycle shop and asked for Smitty, the man he'd talked to the day before. "Did you make up your mind about selling the bike?" Smitty asked the minute he saw Jack.

"Offer me five hundred bucks more, and you've got yourself a deal."

"Okay, man, you got it. Let's take care of the pulp."

Jack blinked. "Come again?"

"The paperwork, man." He motioned for Jack to follow him inside an office. He paused at the door. "By the way, how come you want to sell your chopper? I mean it's a fine piece of machinery, and you've taken good care of it."

"I want to buy a station wagon," Jack said dully.

The man nodded, as though it made perfect sense. "A wagon, huh? Gee, I don't know much about wagons."

"Neither do I."

"What do you plan to do with it?"

"Get married."

"Oh, I got it. Your bride don't like bikes."

"She doesn't like my jeans or my earring either."

"Hey, that's a bummer, man."

Jack shook his head. "Not when you love somebody."

"Okay, call out the next number," Ashley told Chip, her finger poised in midair as she waited to dial.

Chip rolled his eyes and sighed. "Mom, we've been

calling for an hour now. Do you realize how many motorcycle shops there are in Atlanta?"

"There are fewer motorcycle shops than doughnut shops," she quipped, and didn't offer an explanation when Chip looked at her as though she'd lost her mind. "I just wish Uncle Jeeter had remembered the name of the place. If Jack sells that bike, I'll never forgive myself."

"What has selling the bike got to do with you?"

"It has everything to do with me. I have this awful habit of trying to make people into something they're not."

It was obvious Chip had no idea what she was talking about, but he didn't try to question her further. "Let me dial," he said, taking the phone from her trembling hands. "You look up the numbers." He punched the telephone numbers as she called them out.

When a man answered on the other end, he repeated the spiel they had since memorized. "I know this is a stupid question," he began, "but have you had anybody in your shop today by the name of Jack Sloan? We were told he was going to try and sell his motorcycle today, a Harley Davidson." Chip held his hand over the phone. "I don't believe I'm doing this. Do you know what our chances are of finding Jack this way? Zilch, I tell you." He spelled it. "Z-I-L-C-H."

"You don't have to spell it for me. I used to be a librarian, remember?"

"Hello?" Chip's eyes widened. "You do? He is?" He covered the mouthpiece. "Jack's there right now! This minute!"

"Get him on the phone," she said excitedly.

Once the call was transferred to the office that
Jack was supposed to be in, another man picked up
the telephone. "This is Smitty Smith," the man replied. "You want to talk to who?" He held the phone
out for Jack. "It's for you."

Jack looked surprised. "Who is it?"

He shrugged. "I don't know, man. I'll have to find
out." He spoke into the phone. "Who is this?"

"I'm calling for Ashley Rogers," Chip said.

"He's calling for somebody named Roger, I think
he said."

Jack waved the statement aside. At the moment
he wasn't in the mood to talk to anybody. "I don't
know a Roger. Tell him I can't come to the phone."

"Uh, Mr. Sloan can't come to the telephone right
now—we're discussing business." The man paused
and blinked several times. "What do you mean, don't
sell the bike?" When Jack looked up in question,
the man shrugged. Then Ashley got on the phone
and explained the situation.

Smitty grinned. "I think it's your bride, man. She
says not to sell the bike. She says to tell you she
loves you like you are, and you won't have to wear
polyester pants." He shrugged. "I don't know about
you, man, but she sounds like a fox to me."

"What about the station wagon?" Jack asked,
thinking out loud.

"Hey, how about the station wagon?" Smitty asked
Ashley.

Ashley held her hand over the phone and whispered to Chip. "He's asking something about a station wagon."

"What station wagon?" Chip asked.

"What station wagon?" Ashley echoed to Smitty.

Smitty looked at Jack. "She don't know nothin about no station wagon, man."

"Okay, just ask her—" Jack stood. "I'll ask he myself. Tell her I'm on my way over." He was alread halfway through the door when he spoke.

"Does this mean you ain't selling the bike?" Smitt yelled behind him, but there was no answer. He sai good-bye to Ashley and hung up the telephone.

When Jack pulled into her driveway a half hou later, Ashley was pacing the floor and wringing he hands. She'd sent Chip and Mikie to the movies s she and Jack could have some time alone to talk She was going to tell him once and for all how sh felt. In turn she would demand to know his feelings When he knocked on the front door, Ashley though her heart would leap from her chest.

"Hello, Sherlock," he said when she opened th door. His face was unreadable.

"Come in." She waited until he was inside befor closing the door. "You look good," she said, an meant it. His jeans clung to the muscles in hi thighs and calves and outlined a perfect rear end. I had been less than forty-eight hours since she' seen him, but it seemed like months.

He rocked back and forth on his heels. "You loo pretty good yourself." She was dressed in a short outfit made of terry cloth, and Jack was reminded o how pretty her legs were.

"Jack—" Ashley stepped forward. "I'm sorry I go angry with you about Chip. You were only trying t help, and I appreciate it. It's just, well, I'm not use to having help. I've always done everything myself.

suppose I thought my way was the only way. That doesn't mean I can't change."

"Ashley—"

"And the things you said, you were right," she continued. "I do expect a lot from people. Especially Chip. I didn't want him to turn out like his father. But just because I didn't get along with the man doesn't make him a bad person. I don't know if any of this is making sense. I expected a lot from you, too, but that's because I love you." There, she'd said it.

Jack gazed down tenderly at the woman before him. Although it was plain to see how anxious she was, there was a sparkle in her eyes that spoke of the love she'd just confessed. He couldn't deny himself the pleasure of touching her any more than he could deny himself food and water. What was this crazy thing that existed between them? What was it that made him think of her constantly and want to spend every waking moment with her? And what was it that made him feel so protective toward her and her children?

Jack reached for her and captured her lips with his. The kiss was long and unhurried, a kiss he hoped would prove his feelings. He could not find the adequate words.

When Jack raised his head, Ashley's eyes were still closed. He gathered her closer and pressed his lips to her hair. "If we get married, would you go skinny-dipping with me again?" he asked softly.

Ashley felt sure her heart was about to burst in her chest. There was no other explanation for the love she felt overflowing inside. "Is this a marriage proposal?"

"Damn right it is." He saw the question in her eyes and knew this was one time he'd have to open up to her. After all, he wanted her to become his wife. He would have to learn to trust her with his words and feelings. He supposed he already had to an extent.

"I love you," he whispered. It felt good to finally say it, and it warmed him all over when she smiled in return. It hadn't been so bad after all, he thought, telling her he loved her. In fact, he wanted to do it again.

"I love you, Ashley, and I'd like you to become my wife."

Ashley nodded. "I love you too. And I would be thrilled to be your wife." She had barely got the words out of her mouth before he crushed her in his arms and kissed her till her head spun.

"What do you think your boys will say?" he asked when he raised his head.

"I think they'll be delighted."

"I want to be there for them," he said. "I never thought I'd say something like that. I've changed." He looked at her tenderly. "Falling in love changes a person, doesn't it?"

She kissed the tip of his chin. "Just don't change too much. I've grown rather fond of you the way you are."

"I'll try to be a good husband, I swear. What about children? Babies, to be precise. Are we going to have any?" He held his breath.

"I think it would be wonderful having your baby inside of me. We don't have to do it right away, of course." She saw the uncertainty in his eyes. "You'll make a wonderful father, Jack. It's going to feel different, but you can do it. Why don't we take it slow and easy?"

A wicked gleam filled his eyes. "Slow and easy, huh? I like the sound of that." He glanced around the room. "Where—"

"They're at the movies."

"When—"

"A couple of hours from now."

Without warning he bent over and lifted her high in his arms, amid her cries of protest. "I'll show you slow and easy, lady." He carried her into the bedroom and kicked the door closed behind them.

THE EDITOR'S CORNER

This summer Bantam has not only provided you with a mouth-watering lineup of LOVESWEPTs, but with some excellent women's fiction as well. We wanted to alert you to several terrific books which are available right now from your bookseller.

A few years ago we published a unique, sophisticated love story in the LOVESWEPT line called **AZURE DAYS, QUICKSILVER NIGHTS** by talented author Carole Nelson Douglas. Carole has an incredible imagination, and her idea for her next project just knocked our socks off. Set in Las Vegas, **CRYSTAL DAYS**—a June release—and **CRYSTAL NIGHTS**—a July release—are delightfully entertaining books. Each features two love stories and the crazy character Midnight Louie, who can't be described in mere words. Don't miss these two summer treats.

Speaking of treats, Nora Roberts's long-awaited next book, **PUBLIC SECRETS**, is on the stands! Nora's strengths as a writer couldn't be showcased better than in this riveting novel of romantic suspense. **PUBLIC SECRETS** is summer reading at its very best!

Now, on to the LOVESWEPTs we have in store for you!

Suzanne Forster writes with powerful style about characters who are larger than life. In **THE DEVIL AND MS. MOODY**, LOVESWEPT #414, you'll meet two such characters. Edwina Moody, hot on the trail of a missing heir to a fortune, finds her destiny in the arms of an irresistible rebel named Diablo. Edwina is more than out of her element among a bunch of rough-and-tumble bikers, yet Diablo makes her feel as if she's finally found home. On his own mission, Diablo sees a chance to further both their causes, and he convinces Edwina to make a bargain with the devil himself. You'll soon discover—along with Edwina—that Diablo is somewhat a sheep in wolf's clothing, as he surrenders his heart to the woman who longs to possess him. Much of the impact of this wonderful love story is conveyed through Suzanne's writing. I guarantee you'll want to savor every word!

This month several of our characters find themselves in some pretty desperate situations. In **RELENTLESS**, LOVESWEPT #415 by Patt Bucheister, heroine Dionne Hart takes over the helm of a great business empire—and comes face-to-face once again with the man she'd loved fifteen years

(continued)

before. Nick Lyon remembers the blushing teenager with the stormy eyes, and is captivated by the elegant woman she's become. He's relentless in his pursuit of Dionne, but she can't bring herself to share her secrets with a man she had loved but never trusted, a writer who couldn't do his job and respect her privacy too. But Nick won't take no for an answer and continues to knock down the walls of her resistance until all she can do is give in to her desire. Patt will have you rooting loudly for these two people and for their happiness. If only men like Nick could be cloned!

Talk about a desperate situation! Terry Lawrence certainly puts Cally Baldwin in one in **WANTED: THE PERFECT MAN,** LOVESWEPT #416. What would you do if you'd just dumped the latest in a long line of losers and had made a vow to swear off men—then met a man your heart told you was definitely *the one*! Cally does the logical thing, she decides to be "just friends" with Steve Rousseau. But Cally isn't fooling anyone with her ploy—and Steve knows her sizzling good-night kisses are his proof. He takes his time in wooing her, cultivating her trust and faith in him. Much to his dismay, however, he realizes Cally has more than just a few broken relationships in her past to overcome before he can make her believe in forever. And just when she thinks she's lost him, Cally learns Steve really is her perfect man. All you readers who've yet to find someone who fits your personal wanted poster's description will take heart after reading this lively romance. And those of you who have the perfect man will probably think of a few more qualities to add to his list.

If you've been following the exploits of the group of college friends Tami Hoag introduced in her *Rainbow Chasers* series, you're no doubt awaiting Jayne Jordan's love story. in **REILLY'S RETURN,** LOVESWEPT #417, Jayne finds the answer her heart and soul have been seeking. Since Jayne is quite a special lady, no ordinary man could dream of winning her. It takes the likes of Pat Reilly, the Australian movie star the press has dubbed the Hunk from Down Under, to disturb Jayne's inner peace. As much as she'd like to deny it, all the signs point to the fact that Reilly is her destiny—but that doesn't make the journey into forever with him any less tempestuous. Tami has an innate ability to mix humor with tender sensuality, creating the kind of story you tell us you love so much—one that can make you laugh and

(continued)

make you cry. Don't pass up the opportunity to experience a truly memorable love story in **REILLY'S RETURN.**

At last Joan Elliott Pickart has answered your requests and written Dr. Preston Harper's story! Joan has received more mail about Preston Harper over the years than about any other character, so she wanted to take extra care to give him a special lady love and story all his own. With **PRESTON HARPER, M.D.,** LOVESWEPT #418, Joan fulfills every expectation. As a pediatrician, Preston's love for children is his life's calling, but he longs to be a real dad. The problem is, he doesn't see himself in the role of husband! When Dinah Bradshaw walks into his office with the child who's made her an instant mom, Preston's well-ordered plans suddenly fall flat. But Dinah doesn't want marriage any more than Preston had—she's got a law career to get off the ground. Can you guess what happens to these two careful people when love works its magic on them?

Next in her *SwanSea Place* series is Fayrene Preston's **THE PROMISE,** LOVESWEPT #419. In this powerful story of an impossible love Fayrene keeps you on the edge of your seat, breathless with anticipation as Conall Deverell honors a family promise to Sharon Graham—a promise to make her pregnant! Sharon vows she wants nothing else from the formidable man who'd broken her heart ten years before by claiming that the child she'd carried wasn't his. But neither can control the passion that flares between them as Sharon accepts Conall's challenge to make him want her, make his blood boil. You've come to expect the ultimate in a romance from Fayrene, and she doesn't disappoint with **THE PROMISE!**

Best wishes from the entire LOVESWEPT staff,
Sincerely,

Susann Brailey

Susann Brailey
Editor
LOVESWEPT
Bantam Books
666 Fifth Avenue
New York, NY 10103

FAN OF THE MONTH

Mary Gregg

Reading has always been a part of my life. I come from a long line of readers who consider books treasured friends. I cannot imagine a life without books—how dull and bland it would be.

LOVESWEPTs are *the best* contemporary romances due to one lady, Carolyn Nichols. From the beginning Carolyn promised quality not quantity, and she has kept her promise over the years.

Some of my favorite authors are: Sandra Brown—she must use her husband as a hero model; Kay Hooper, who I can always depend on for her wonderful sense of humor; Iris Johansen; Helen Mittermeyer; Linda Cajio; Billie Green; Joan Elliott Pickart; and Fayrene Preston, who reminds me a little of Shirley Temple.

At the end of the day I can curl up with a LOVESWEPT and transport myself back to the days of my childhood, when Prince Charming and Cinderella were my friends. After all, romance stories are modern fairy tales for grown-ups, in which the characters live happily ever after.

60 Minutes to a Better, More Beautiful You!

Now it's easier than ever to awaken your sensuality, stay slim forever—even make yourself irresistible. With Bantam's bestselling subliminal audio tapes, you're only 60 minutes away from a better, more beautiful you!

__ 45004-2	**Slim Forever**	$8.95
__ 45112-X	**Awaken Your Sensuality**	$7.95
__ 45035-2	**Stop Smoking Forever**	$8.95
__ 45130-8	**Develop Your Intuition**	$7.95
__ 45022-0	**Positively Change Your Life** ...	$8.95
__ 45154-5	**Get What You Want**	$7.95
__ 45041-7	**Stress Free Forever**	$8.95
__ 45106-5	**Get a Good Night's Sleep**	$7.95
__ 45094-8	**Improve Your Concentration** .	$7.95
__ 45172-3	**Develop A Perfect Memory**	$8.95

THE DELANEY DYNASTY

THE SHAMROCK TRINITY

- ☐ 21975 RAFE, THE MAVERICK
  by Kay Hooper $2.95
- ☐ 21976 YORK, THE RENEGADE
  by Iris Johansen $2.95
- ☐ 21977 BURKE, THE KINGPIN
  by Fayrene Preston $2.95

THE DELANEYS OF KILLAROO

- ☐ 21872 ADELAIDE, THE ENCHANTRESS
  by Kay Hooper $2.75
- ☐ 21873 MATILDA, THE ADVENTURESS
  by Iris Johansen $2.75
- ☐ 21874 SYDNEY, THE TEMPTRESS
  by Fayrene Preston $2.75

THE DELANEYS: *The Untamed Years*

- ☐ 21899 GOLDEN FLAMES *by Kay Hooper* $3.50
- ☐ 21898 WILD SILVER *by Iris Johansen* $3.50
- ☐ 21897 COPPER FIRE *by Fayrene Preston* $3.50

THE DELANEYS II

- ☐ 21978 SATIN ICE *by Iris Johansen* $3.50
- ☐ 21979 SILKEN THUNDER *by Fayrene Preston* $3.50
- ☐ 21980 VELVET LIGHTNING *by Kay Hooper* $3.50

THE LATEST IN BOOKS
AND AUDIO CASSETTES

Paperbacks

☐	28416	**RIGHTFULLY MINE** Doris Mortman	$5.95
☐	27032	**FIRST BORN** Doris Mortman	$4.95
☐	27283	**BRAZEN VIRTUE** Nora Roberts	$3.95
☐	25891	**THE TWO MRS. GRENVILLES** Dominick Dunne	$4.95
☐	27891	**PEOPLE LIKE US** Dominick Dunne	$4.95
☐	27260	**WILD SWAN** Celeste De Blasis	$4.95
☐	25692	**SWAN'S CHANCE** Celeste De Blasis	$4.50
☐	26543	**ACT OF WILL** Barbara Taylor Bradford	$5.95
☐	27790	**A WOMAN OF SUBSTANCE** Barbara Taylor Bradford	$5.95
☐	27197	**CIRCLES** Doris Mortman	$4.95

Audio

☐ **THE SHELL SEEKERS** by Rosamunde Pilcher
Performance by Lynn Redgrave
180 Mins. Double Cassette   48183-9 $14.95

☐ **COLD SASSY TREE** by Olive Ann Burns
Performance by Richard Thomas
180 Mins. Double Cassette   45166-9 $14.95

☐ **PEOPLE LIKE US** by Dominick Dunne
Performance by Len Cariou
180 Mins. Double Cassette   45164-2 $14.95

☐ **CAT'S EYE** by Margaret Atwood
Performance by Kate Nelligan
180 Mins. Double Cassette   45203-7 $14.95

Bantam Books, Dept. FBS, 414 East Golf Road, Des Plaines, IL 60016

Please send me the items I have checked above. I am enclosing $_____
(please add $2.00 to cover postage and handling). Send check or money
order, no cash or C.O.D.s please. (Tape offer good in USA only.)

Mr/Ms _____

Address _____

City/State _____ Zip _____

Please allow four to six weeks for delivery.

Prices and availability subject to change without notice.

FBS-8/90